SURVIVE THE FALL

DARK ROADS

DEREK SHUPERT

ALSO BY DEREK SHUPERT

SURVIVE THE FALL SERIES:
POWERLESS WORLD
MADNESS RISING
DARK ROADS

THE COMPLETE DEAD STATE SERIES:
DEAD STATE: CATALYST (PREQUEL)
DEAD STATE: FALLOUT
DEAD STATE: SURVIVAL ROAD
DEAD STATE: EXECUTIONER
DEAD STATE: IMMUNE
DEAD STATE: EVOLVED

THE COMPLETE DEAD STATE SERIES BOX SET

THE COMPLETE AFFLICTED SERIES:
GENESIS (PREQUEL)
PATIENT ZERO
RIPTIDE
DEAD RECKONING

THE HUNTRESS BANE SERIES:
THE HUNTRESS BANE (SHORT STORY)
TAINTED HUNTER
CRIMSON THIRST

THE COMPLETE BALLISTIC MECH SERIES:
DIVISION
INFERNO
EXTINCTION
PAYBACK

STAND ALONE
SENTRY SQUAD

DEDICATION

I wouldn't be able to write without those who support me. I thank you for your encouragement and being there for me.

To those that read my books, I thank you for your support.

CHAPTER ONE

SARAH

S arah stood on the pier in Boston's harbor, facing the masked man that rescued her from the Irish mob who looked to kidnap her.

He reached for Sarah, grabbing her forearm with a firm grip. The white ghost skull imprinted on the face of the black fabric made him look menacing–intimidating. "You need to come with me now, Sarah, while there's still time."

Sarah wrenched her arm from his hand, then clipped his jaw with her balled fist. Even though he saved her from the Irish mob, he had no place to grab her in such a way. "Like hell I am, Spencer. You might be wearing that mask, but your voice doesn't lie."

The glancing blow knocked him back on his heels. The gun lowered and trained at her side. He shook his head, rubbed his jaw, then cut his narrowed eyes up to her.

"I don't want to harm you, Sarah. I love you," he said, training his piece at her once more. "But I'll do whatever is needed to keep you safe, even if you can't see it. Now let's go before–"

A muffled report of gunfire sounded from the warehouse next to them.

Sarah ducked, then looked to the open door of the large building built on the pier in Boston's harbor.

He peered over his shoulder–checking the side entrance for any threats.

Sarah glanced down at Samuel Kinnerk's pistol, her former captor. The Irish mob boss had been shot by Spencer who stood in disguise before her.

She inched forward, reaching for the weapon.

He doubled down on her. "Please, don't do that, my love."

Sarah froze with her arm extended toward the weapon. "Stop saying that. I'm not your love or anything else, you whack job."

"We're meant to be together, and one day, you will accept that reality. Now let's–"

A rush of loud, angry voices echoed through the open door of the warehouse.

Spencer shifted his attention to the growing clamor of shouting and footfalls that sounded from the warehouse–drawing closer to their position. "No, no, no."

Sarah dropped to the wooden planks in a blink and reached for Samuel's pistol. She grabbed the sidearm and rolled to her side.

Spencer spun on the heels of his boots and fired at two of Kinnerk's men who materialized from the warehouse. One went down with a shot to the head–crumbling to the pier, lifeless.

Sarah scrambled to her feet as Spencer and the lone surviving henchman dueled. She kept low and flinched from each gunshot. Sarah peered over her shoulder, catching brief flashes of muzzle fire.

2

Dark Roads

The pistol held firm in her hand. Sarah gathered her footing and found cover behind a pile of weathered and deteriorating pallets. She craned her neck around the edge of the splintered wood and watched the shootout.

Spencer fired at a large red-bearded man until his pistol ran dry. He ejected the spent magazine and slapped in a fresh mag in one fluid motion. He continued firing at the henchman concealed behind a crate to the side of the entrance.

Sarah skimmed over the pier in the opposite direction, finding more stacks of pallets, crates, and other junk that lined the outside of the building. If she kept low and moved quick, she might be able to slip away.

Indecision racked her, though. Mandy, her best friend, was trapped in the middle of the hailstorm of gunfire that both men shelled out. Sarah thought she was alive, but couldn't tell through the chaos.

Damn it.

Spencer took two direct hits to the chest that sent him stumbling backward. He fell flat on his ass, then onto his back. He laid motionless on the pier–showing no signs of life.

Sarah searched for the last remaining threat. She spotted movement within the crates. Red poked his head out from around the corner, then stood up. He ejected his magazine and dug his hand into his back pants pocket.

Sarah leaned away from the pallets a hair more and stared in the direction of Philip, Samuel's large goon who draped over Mandy's body.

The gun.

Sarah squeezed the grip of Samuel's pistol a hair tighter. She took two quick breaths, then stepped away from her cover.

Red turned her way and aimed his gun.

Sarah squeezed the trigger.

Samuel's piece clicked empty.

Red opened fire, sending Sarah reeling for cover. Wood splintered with each round that punched the fragile, decaying timber.

"Come out, Mrs. Cage," Red said, in his thick Irish accent. "You have no place to go."

Sarah toed the edge of the battered boards, watching Red head her way.

A single shot fired from Spencer, prone on his back.

The bullet struck Red in the ribs and sent him scurrying for cover.

Spencer turned his head, then looked her way. He sat up from the pier with his piece trained at the open doorway. "Sarah."

Red popped off another round that skimmed past Spencer's ghost mask.

He flinched, ducked, then returned fire.

Sarah didn't want to leave Mandy behind, but with an empty gun and armed threats before her, she had no choice but to flea while she could.

She bolted from the pallets in a fit of grief and rage.

Spencer got to his feet–firing as he stood and backed away.

How did he survive that? Is he wearing a bullet-proof vest or something? Sarah thought.

Her feet hammered the pier. She ran as hard and fast as her legs would take her, not daring to look back.

The gunfire lessened the farther she drifted from the battle. She kept the pistol trained ahead, a deterrent to those who stood in her way, and searched for any incoming threats.

Sarah neared the edge of the warehouse. Both hands held the grip taut. She snaked along the stacks of boxes and crates. She toed the blind corner and scoped out the area.

Dark Roads

Three SUV's sat parked at the end of the warehouse. Their doors hung wide open, but she didn't spot any movement in or around the vehicles. She looked to the other end of the warehouse, and found an armed man with his back to her.

He turned and glanced her way, then leaned back on the heels of his black boots.

She caught a glimpse of the rifle clutched in his gloved hands.

Sarah retreated back behind the cover of the warehouse. She deflated against the steel siding of the building. Her head dangled toward the weathered wooden planks. She wiped the sweat from across her brow, then flicked her hand. Her mind raced, making it hard to focus on escaping.

Come on. Come on, think.

She took in a deep breath, ventured another look, and found the armed man absent from his post.

Sarah crouched, then ran from the cover of the building to the SUV closest to her. Raised voices loomed from the far side of the warehouse. She skirted the open driver's side door and down the length of the vehicle, stopping at the rear.

The men drew closer to the SUV. Their muttered, angry voices grew louder.

"Where is Samuel Kinnerk?" one of the men asked. His deep, baritone voice boomed like angry thunder and filled with rage. Sarah shuddered. "I want him found and brought to me, now. Anyone else you can silence, but Kinnerk and the two women are to be left unharmed."

The report of gunfire echoed in the dismal gray sky, then ebbed. She slipped around the bumper, turned, then peered down the long stretch of pier that led to the back entrance of the warehouse.

Spencer vanished from sight. Kinnerk's men had disappeared as well.

Where is he? Sarah thought, hoping he might've caught a bullet that took him down and given her one less problem to contend with.

Two men, dressed in black tactical garb, hustled toward the corner of the warehouse with rifles shouldered. They paused for a moment, checking the blind corner for any threats, then slipped around the back of the building, and moved down the pier side by side.

Sarah watched the men sweeping the junk piled alongside the exterior of the warehouse. Their attention was focused ahead of them and not on the empty SUV's.

She turned toward the street that connected to the dock–finding it clear of any armed men. A row of buildings sat on the other side of the road. She could make it if she ran fast enough.

Sarah stood from her crouched position, then peered through the rear window of the SUV.

A figure stood near the front of the vehicle just past the open passenger side door. A portion of the SUV concealed his face, leaving only the black tactical gear and gloves he wore visible.

Who the hell are these guys?

He set his piece on the SUV, slammed his fist on the hood, then turned toward the windshield. His forearms rested on the vehicle, his head hanging in frustration. He ran his hand over his face, then over the top of his shaved head.

Sarah caught a glimpse of the burnt flesh that resided on the side of his face. The skin looked coarse–leathery even. It made him look more monster than man.

He lifted his head, then glanced her way.

Dark Roads

Sarah dipped below the edge of the window. Her heart hammered against her chest. She waited a moment, raised up, and glanced through the bottom portion of the dingy window again.

Static hissed and crackled from the two-way radio he clutched. He lifted the radio to his mouth, shaking his head.

"Team two, report," Leatherface said. He tilted his head to the side, training an attentive ear to the speaker. No response came. He adjusted the dials on the top of the radio, then said, "Johnson, Bennet, what's the situation back there? Over."

The report of gunfire tainted the air. It sounded muffled and restricted, then died off.

A distorted voice broke through the constant crackling and white noise, making it hard to hear what they said.

Leatherface tweaked the signal some more, clearing the distortion out.

"We've got two bodies–Kinnerk's men," the voice replied. The voice sounded robotic. "Blood… heading… building."

What? Only two bodies identified as Kinnerk's men. They didn't mention Mandy. Did that mean she survived or escaped?

Leatherface continued adjusting the dials on the top of the radio, trying to clear up the garbled signal. He retrieved his pistol from the hood, then walked around the front of the SUV. He held the radio close to his ear and made for the corner of the warehouse. Despite moving away from the vehicle, she could still hear his voice as if he stood next to her.

"I don't give a crap about his dead men," Leatherface said, shouting into the two-way radio. "Those two females and Kinnerk's head are worth a lot of money, so if you value your lives, find them, now."

Sarah peered around the edge of the SUV, watching Leatherface.

He stood with his back to her, staring down the long stretch of pier with his piece at his side. The radio stayed close to his ear as he craned his neck and shifted his weight.

Sarah backed away from the SUV, watching Leatherface's every move. His attention remained focused dead ahead.

She turned about face and took off in a dead sprint. Her feet hammered the wooden planks of the pier. She made for the road. Sarah skimmed over the buildings, searching for a way through the solid wall of metal that spanned down both sides of the road. It looked to be more warehouses with roll up doors lining their fronts.

The armed men yelled in her direction.

Gunfire crackled in the sky behind her. A warning shot that went wide, missing her by a mile. She flinched, lowered her head, and kept running.

Sarah peered over her shoulder, nearing the end of the pier.

Leatherface pointed in her direction while barking at two of his men chasing her down. They skirted past the SUVs with their rifles clutched in their hands.

A narrow gap within the buildings presented itself ahead of Sarah. It looked like a tight fit, but large enough for her frame to slip through.

She ran hard and fast for the opening.

The armed men gained on her–their footfalls growing louder.

Sarah slipped through the narrow passage, then ran down the long corridor. If she had any hopes of surviving, she had to lose them, and fast.

CHAPTER TWO

RUSSELL

The day's events had taken its toll on Russell, wearing him down beyond the point of exhaustion. He hadn't realized how damaged he was until he stopped moving.

Every inch of his body ached.

The muscles in his legs throbbed.

His ankle radiated pain.

Each breath he took made his ribs hurt.

It was all par for the course. Moving through the rugged terrain of the Blue Ridge Mountains for the past few days had been no small feat, even for those in top form. But recovering from a plane crash and a hostile encounter with crooked police and backwoods rejects was bound to prolong any expected recovery. He didn't consider himself a slouch, but he wasn't in peak physical condition either.

Russell adjusted himself in the seat of the Bronco, trying to find comfort any way he could.

His eyes grew thick with sleep. A yawn attacked him, forcing his mouth open. His eyelids clamped shut, pushing the wetness out both tear ducts.

"You all right?" Cathy asked, slouched in the passenger seat with her boots resting on the cracked dash. "Do you need me to drive for a bit? I don't mind. It's the least I can do."

Russell shook his head, then blinked, erasing the sheen from his vision. "I'm good. Just tired and sore is all. If I get too comfortable, I'll be out. I need to stay alert. Besides, you're a better navigator than I would be."

Max, Cathy's German shepherd, rested in the back on the bench seat. His front paws dangled from the edge of the worn tan leather. He stared at Russell with his large, brown eyes, then yawned. His jaws opened wide, revealing his fangs.

Cathy folded the map in her lap, then sat up straight in the seat. "I'm not one to beat a dead horse by any means, and I know I've already thanked you, but I do appreciate everything you've done for Max and me. I can't say that too many folks would have gone up against Marcus Wright and his goons. Lord knows no one had except for me. Anyway, thanks again for not bailing on us. You're a good man. Your wife is pretty lucky to have you, Cage."

Russell offered a warm smile, then nodded. She didn't have to keep thanking him, considering she saved his life first from that mountain lion that sought to make a meal of him, but Cathy did nonetheless. She had a generous and kind soul. One that made her go out of her way for him when he needed it most.

"I appreciate the kind words. All of them. But don't worry, I have no plans of holding any of what I did over your head," Russell replied, smirking.

Dark Roads

Cathy guffawed, then folded her arms across her chest. "Somebody thinks they're funny."

Russell shrugged, then winced from a subtle pain in his ribs. His hand pressed against his side with a gentle touch. "Funny might be a stretch, but I try."

"All right, funny man." Cathy peered at his side, erasing the warm smile off her face. "Ribs hurting?"

"Yeah, along with everything else, but I'll live," Russell answered. "How far did you say it was again to Philadelphia?"

Cathy pointed through the windshield to the open road. They hadn't seen any other vehicles for the past hour or so. "It's about two hundred twenty-nine miles I believe. Taking the I-66 E route should buy us a bit of time. If we maintain our current pace, limit our stops to just one, two if needed, and the roads remain clear like they are, we should be there in about three hours or so."

Max poked his head between the seats, nudging Cathy's arm with his nose.

"Hey, you." She reached across her body and rubbed the crown of his head, giving him some well-deserved attention. "How's my big boy doing?"

Max tilted his head back, then flicked his pink tongue at Cathy's cheek.

Russell's stomach growled, snapping the German shepherd's attention in his direction.

"Hungry?" Cathy rubbed behind Max's ears, massaging the soft spot at the base.

"You could say that." The mere mention of food made Russell's stomach more restless. His mouth felt parched—gums tacky to the touch. He needed a drink of water, among other things. "Why don't we make one stop, gather up the supplies we need, and push through to Philly? If we do that, we should be good. Plus, I imagine Max is pretty thirsty and hungry, aren't you?"

Max sniffed in Russell's direction, then flicked his tongue out.

Cathy gave the canine a kiss on the head, then faced forward. "That sounds good. There should be a mom and pop gas station coming up soon if I remember correctly. It's been some time since I've taken this drive. My late husband, Bill, liked to fly when we went to visit Amber in Philly. I preferred the freedom of the open road. He'd always say, 'Why waste time driving when we could get to our daughter faster by plane?'"

Russell looked over the fuel gauge on the dash, then said, "Probably wouldn't hurt to fuel up if we can. This truck is drinking fuel like crazy."

"We'll see if we can get some gas wherever we stop. Hopefully, they'll have a backup generator running the pumps."

Russell spotted a blue-tinted sign on the side of the road with an image of a gas pump imprinted on the front. "Looks like we might be in luck. Keep your eyes peeled."

They cruised along I-66 for a bit longer, scouting the area for the gas station. Any homes or businesses they passed showed no signs of power. The interior of the structures beyond the windows loomed dark and endless.

The sun dipped below the horizon, bringing forth another night of pure blackness. Thick, bulbous clouds hung overhead like a shroud. They'd be hard pressed to see the moon's gleam or stars twinkling in the sky.

Russell cranked his window down, allowing the cool breeze to funnel inside the cab. The noise and nip of the wind brushing against his face kept him alert.

Dark Roads

Cathy rapped her hand against Russell's arm, then pointed out the windshield. "Looks like there's a Shell station coming up. Sign isn't lit, though."

"It's better than nothing. Worst case, we'll move on to the next station," Russell replied, shrugging his shoulders.

Max sat on his haunches at attention–focusing on the road ahead. He groaned, then pawed at the seat.

Russell slowed the Bronco as they neared the station. He didn't spot any cars in or around the building. There weren't any other houses or businesses along the highway either.

"I wonder if they're even open."

Cathy shrugged. "No clue. We can stop to see. Worst case, they're not, and we'll move on, like you said."

Russell thumbed the blinker, then turned down the concrete drive. They pulled alongside the older looking pumps and stopped. He placed the truck into park, killed the engine, then removed the keys from the ignition. "Well, I guess we'll at least go up to the door, and see if they're open."

"There's a car parked on the far side of the building. You see the bumper?" Cathy pointed out the cream-colored bumper of the sedan that protruded from the corner of the station.

"Yeah. Could be abandoned, though." Russell tugged on the door handle, then pushed the door open. The hinges squeaked.

He slipped out of the driver's seat to the cement, then slammed his door shut.

The stiffness in his legs caused him to walk with a slight limp at first. Russell stretched and rubbed his thighs, then continued on.

Cathy and Max got out on the other side.

Russell made his way around the back end of the Bronco. Max greeted him with a sharp bark and wag of his tail.

Cathy studied the pumps, leaning close to the dust-covered plastic fronts. Her hand swiped over the dirt. A disgusted look washed over her face. "These pumps are old school. They have the numbers that flip over."

"If they work, it doesn't matter, right?" Russell asked, petting Max's head.

"True, but I'm skeptical that their age will be the worst of our problems."

Russell nodded at the building. "Let's go see if we can get some water and food. As much as I'd love a thick, juicy hamburger right now with a mound of hot, crispy fries, I'd take some candy bars and chips."

Max licked his lips from the mere mention of the delectable treats.

"I think I'm going to see if the bathroom over there is unlocked. I've been holding it for a while." Cathy passed between the faded-white gas pumps and made for the far corner of the station near the cream-colored sedan.

"Looks like it's you and me again, bud." Russell rubbed the top of Max's head who trotted along at his side.

Cathy veered toward the corner of the station as Max and Russell approached the front glass door.

Russell read the name of the business on the bulkhead fixed to the top of the building.

Debbie's Gas and Gulp.

Max lowered his head and stared at the darkness beyond the glass door. He didn't growl or offer any sort of warning indicating that a threat lingered within the dull light.

Russell leaned close to the door, then placed the ridge of his hand above his brow. What little bit of light remained from outside penetrated only so far.

Dark Roads

The open sign to the side of the door had no power. No other indicators hinted that the station was closed, or open for that matter.

"Hello?" Russell knocked on the glass, waiting for a response. None came. "Is anyone in there?"

He waited a bit longer for a reply, but there was nothing more than dead silence.

The shelves closest to the door were stocked with an array of sugary treats that made his mouth water. A mixture of Snickers, Milky Way, and Butterfingers could be seen.

Russell grabbed the silver metal handle on the door and pulled. It opened without restriction.

Max waited at the gap for Russell to open it far enough for him to slip inside.

"Keep your eyes peeled and ears open, bud." Russell opened the door farther, allowing Max to take the lead and venture inside.

The hinges on the door creaked the more Russell moved it.

The air was stagnant and hot.

Silence filled the store with no audible sounds to hint anyone lurked within the ether.

Max trained his nose to the black and white checkered linoleum tile floor and investigated. He sniffed along, then hooked down one of the rows between the shelves.

Russell skimmed over the rows of shelves stocked with food and other nonperishable items. Along the far side wall, coolers ran the width of the building, then down the back wall. From what he could see, it looked to have an assortment of drinks jammed into the slanted shelves.

A flashlight would be nice right now, Russell thought. He didn't want to power on his phone unless necessary. It hadn't been charged in some time, and the last time he checked there was little to no power left.

Look for a portable battery pack.

He logged the mental note in his head, then made his way to the checkout counter. "If anyone is here, we're looking to get some food, drinks, gas, and any other supplies. We'll pay for what we take."

Russell didn't receive a response, making him wonder where the clerk resided.

The cluttered space behind the counter looked empty. A plastic crate, boxes, and other items sat on the floor. He couldn't spot any lights, or other markers to signal that the fuel pumps were working.

Crap.

Russell grabbed a plastic sack from near the counter, then turned toward the shelves.

Max milled about the store, sniffing any food that piqued his interest. He lingered at the beef jerky. Good choice.

Russell shopped the store, grabbing any and all items that he could stuff inside the sack. It bulged at the sides, testing the strength of the plastic. He opened a package of jerky and fed it to Max.

The German shepherd snatched it from his hand and consumed the meaty treat in a blink.

Oh. What do we have here?

A small section of the shelves toward the front of the store, near the register, had a small supply of liquor on the top shelf.

The bottles filled Russell's gaze, tormenting him to pop open their tops and partake. His mouth watered at the thought. The urge to take a single sip grew stronger the more he lingered in front of the bottles.

Russell grabbed a bottle of Jack Daniels, stuffed it inside the front pocket of his jeans, and moved on.

Dark Roads

A small display of electronic items caught his eye. The black shroud hanging over the display made it hard to see. He leaned in close, searching for a portable battery charger.

Max growled under his breath. The German shepherd stood rigid in the main aisle, facing the entrance to the convenience store. Even through the dimness, Russell could see and sense the tension swelling in the canine's large frame.

The grumbling of an engine from outside the store caught Russell's ear, followed by the skidding of tires over the pavement. He couldn't spot the vehicle from where he stood, but he knew what caused the sound.

Great.

CHAPTER THREE

RUSSELL

Max inched his way toward the entrance of the convenience store. Both ears stood erect, and his tail was taut. He growled under his breath, searching for the source of his anxiousness.

Russell flanked the canine, craning his neck to see the blind spot beyond the corner of the glass door.

A jacked-up brown Chevy truck sat in the parking lot, away from the building. It wasn't parked near any pumps or anything else for that matter. Strange.

The front of the truck had clumps of mud covering the front. The grill and bumper had chunks of grass clinging to the frame. A thick layer of dried dirt coated the windshield, leaving only the path where the wipers ran visible.

Hillbillies. Awesome.

Dark Roads

Russell didn't spot Cathy, making him more anxious. He glanced over what little he could see of the parking lot and near the Bronco. She was nowhere to be found.

A tall, slender man materialized from the corner of the glass door.

Max growled, then lowered to the ground. Russell grabbed him by the collar and held firm.

The door swung open.

Max barked a warning.

The man paused just shy of the threshold. He took a step back from Max. "That is one mean looking pup, there."

The bill of his green John Deere hat pointed at the sky. His jaw worked the toothpick clutched between his teeth. The scraggy hairs growing from the sides of his face were thick and long, and his clothes were dingy, torn, and ragged.

An awful smell of onions radiated from the man's unclean body, assaulting Russell's senses. Russell crinkled his nose as he wrestled with the agitated canine.

Max bared his fangs at the stranger. He pressed forward, trying to get free of Russell's grip around his collar.

John Deere dipped his chin to Max, then glanced up at Russell. "Not sure why your dog is so bent out of shape, friend, but I'd make sure to keep a firm grasp on that collar."

"Max, settle down," Russell said, patting him on the side. He tugged on the collar, pulling him back from the entrance of the store and away from the man. "It's okay, boy."

"Yeah, boy. It's ok," John Deere replied, removing the toothpick and spitting a mouthful of saliva to the ground. It hit the floor like wet cement.

Russell backed away with Max, who was less than cooperative. "Sorry about that. He's pretty protective."

John Deere whipped the thin line of spit that clung to his bottom lip with the back of his hand. "German shepherds are great guard dogs for sure. They can get one hell of a temper, though."

Max calmed on the growling, but he remained vigilant, watching the man's every move.

"Doing some shopping there, friend?" John Deere walked inside the store, closing the door behind him. He eyed the plastic sack stuffed to the gills with food and other items.

Russell looked to the sack, then back to John Deere. "Uh, yeah. I'm not sure where the clerk is, though. We spotted the car on the other side of the building, and the door was unlocked. I grabbed some supplies and planned to leave money on the counter for whatever we took."

"We?" John Deere nodded, then said, "Oh, you must be talking about that tasty little number outside. She's easy on the eyes for sure. You're a lucky man." An unsettling grin formed on the man's face.

Russell shifted his weight between his legs, nostrils flaring. The muscles in his arms twitched, then flexed. He didn't care for the tone or coy smile.

Russell had his Glock 17 concealed in the waistband of his pants behind his back. He contemplated reaching for the weapon, but didn't want to escalate matters further.

"Don't worry, friend, she's in good hands. My friend is keeping her company," John Deere said, smiling.

"Stay, Max." Russell let go of the collar, then removed his wallet from his back pocket. He pulled out a wad of cash and tossed it on the counter near the register.

Max remained poised to strike—lowered to the floor, watching the surly man as subtle growls rumbled from his core.

John Deere lifted his arm and pointed at the counter, revealing the piece tucked his waistband. "You know, some people might constitute what you're doing right there as stealing. Afterall, someone could take that money, then no one would ever know the food and supplies you're taking had been paid for."

"People will think what they want then, I guess." Russell patted his leg and made for the door. "Come on, boy."

He walked around the man with Max trailing behind him.

"Hey, I don't think we're done chatting, pal." John Deere said, raising his voice in frustration.

Russell pushed open the door, leaving the stifling heat of the store and the stench of the foul-smelling man behind him.

John Deere trailed the both of them outside, mumbling under his breath.

Cathy stood next to the stranger's truck, speaking with John Deere's cohort.

"Hey, pal. It's rude to walk away from someone when they're speaking to you," John Deere said. "We don't take kindly to that sort of thing around here, or stealing. Perhaps you need a lesson in manners."

The man standing in front of Cathy had her pressed against the driver's side of the truck. He leaned on the hood, smiling and looking her up and down.

The Corona cap he wore looked in dire shape. The dark navy-blue bill was tattered and frayed. Long, black, wiry strands of hair snaked out from under the cap like spider legs. His thick, bushy, black beard concealed his mouth. The smirched rags he wore looked just as bad as his buddy's–dirty and ripped.

Cathy eyed Russell, then turned away from Corona.

"Hey, where you going? We were just getting to know each other." Corona tossed his hands in the air, looking at Cathy as she walked away.

"Seems like we have some rude thieves in our midst," John Deere said, from behind Russell. "Seems like these out of town folks don't care for conversation or the law."

"Are you ok?" Russell asked, walking alongside Cathy. "They didn't try anything, did they?"

She peered over her shoulder at the two men, then said, "I'm good. It's not the first time I've had to deal with some backwoods hillbillies. Though, I'm glad you came out when you did."

"Yeah. Seems like they're out looking for trouble. I grabbed what I could, and decided to leave when I spotted John Deere's piece tucked in his pants," Russell replied, eyeing the Bronco.

"Can you believe these two?" John Deer said, walking behind them. "I think it might be our civic duty to handle this. What do you think, Boyd?"

"I think you're right, Ned. I do believe it is our duty to protect our little community from such outside trash as these two," Boyd replied.

Max stopped, turned toward John Deere, then barked.

Cathy whirled around and grabbed him by the collar. "Max. Come on, boy. It's not worth it. Let's just go."

Russell spun on his heels, facing the two men. The dying light made it cumbersome to see, but the surge of adrenalin pushed him past any fatigue and helped him focus.

Ned yanked the piece from the front of his jeans, then trained the barrel at Max's forehead. "I already told your friend to control that damn mutt. I'd hate to have to put him down."

The German shepherd lunged forward, baring his fangs and barking at the two men. Cathy wrestled the excited canine, holding him at bay as best she could.

Dark Roads

"Listen. We don't want any trouble here. I paid for what items I took, so nothing's been stolen. We'll be on our way." Russell looked at Ned, then over to Boyd who stood in front of his truck.

"I'll tell you what. How's about that pretty thing right there do the apologizing for the both of you with her mouth," Boyd said, straight-faced while looking at Cathy.

Not going to happen.

Ned looked over to Boyd. His piece drifted to the side some.

Max broke free of Cathy's hold, charging John Deere.

"Look out," Boyd shouted, pointing at Max.

Ned pulled the trigger without looking.

Cathy gasped as fire spat from the barrel.

She turned as the bullet zipped past her leg.

Max leapt, latching onto Ned's forearm–the one that wielded the gun.

Ned bellowed. "Ah. Get this damn animal off me, Boyd."

Corona reached for the top of his pants, feeling around the waistband.

Russell whipped his Glock 17 out from behind his back.

A warning shot fired over the top of the truck, sending Boyd scurrying for cover on the driver's side of the vehicle. He dropped the weapon, then kicked the piece toward the building.

Max thrashed his head and pulled, fighting to take Ned to the pavement.

Ned struggled to keep upright, feet moving in every direction to sustain his balance. He leaned forward and reached for his piece on the pavement, but couldn't take hold of the weapon.

"Max. Let go. Now." Cathy grabbed him by the collar and tugged.

The German shepherd locked in and refused to let go.

Ned wailed, then punched Max in the side, trying to free himself.

Cathy decked Ned in the face while Russell kept Boyd pinned down behind his truck. John Deere stumbled backward. Max released his hold on the man's ravaged arm.

Cathy pulled him away.

"Get in the Bronco, now." Russell trained the Glock at Boyd, then Ned. "We're going to leave. Neither of you will follow us. Am I understood?"

Cathy limped away with Max at her side.

Ned cradled his injured arm, gnashing his teeth and breathing heavily.

Boyd stayed hidden behind his truck. "Ned. You all right?"

"That damn dog chewed my arm up." Blood dripped from his trembling hand to the pavement. The skin on his forearm looked like ground beef–mangled and gnawed on. He stared at the torn flesh with wide eyes, then flitted his gaze back to Russell. "Mark my words, you're going to get yours."

"No, we are not. This is done." Russell lowered to the ground to grab Ned's piece from the pavement. The supplies in the plastic bag shifted. His fingers grazed the grip, then took hold. Russell secured the piece in the front of his pants then backed toward the gas pumps.

Cathy got Max stowed in the backseat, then climbed into the passenger seat.

Russell trained the Glock at the front passenger tire of the truck. He popped off a single round, blowing out the large, thick-treaded tire.

"What the hell?" Boyd yelled.

Ned eyed Russell, hunched over and palming the damaged flesh of his arm.

Dark Roads

Boyd peered around the edge of the truck, then glanced at the front of the building.

Russell forgot he had the keys to the Bronco stuffed in the front of his pants.

Boyd bolted from his cover and made for his piece.

Russell skirted the back end of the Bronco and fished his keys out. The door hung open, waiting for him to get inside. He shoved the bag into the cab, then hopped in.

"Go, go!" Cathy motioned with her hands to speed up.

Max clawed at the window, growling and barking.

The muffled report of gunfire crackled outside.

A single round pinged off the body of the Bronco.

"Christ. Don't they see the damn gas pumps?"

Russell slipped the keys into the ignition, then fired it up.

The engine roared as more incoming fire pelted the exterior of the Bronco.

"Hold on." Russell shifted into drive, then punched the gas.

The back tires squealed. The Bronco tore ass away from the pumps, heading for the highway.

Boyd materialized around the bed of his truck, firing. The orange flashes acted like a beacon, allowing Russell to locate him.

Bullets punched into the front passenger fender as they pulled onto I-66. Russell kept his foot mashed to the floor, pushing the Bronco down the highway until the station faded into the distance.

"Everybody good?" he asked, checking the rear-view mirror.

Cathy palmed her thigh, gritting her teeth.

Even in the dim light, Russell spotted the wetness on her leg. "You've been shot."

Derek Shupert

CHAPTER FOUR

SARAH

The maze of buildings went on forever, making it hard for Sarah to find her way out. At each blind corner, she feared what might be waiting around the bend. She thought on the fly and braved the unknown, unable to rest or think with a clear mind. The armed men stalking her wouldn't allow it.

Her chest tightened, and her lungs hurt. The muscles in her legs burned. Sarah breathed heavily and fought through the pain that racked her tired body. She wanted to stop and rest, but couldn't. Not until she lost her tail.

The footfalls of the mysterious armed men receded, but she could still hear them. Their voices carried in the silence of the harbor, giving her markers to their position.

The discomfort trolling her lower half grew by the second. The fiery prod probing her thighs increased with every step she took, making it harder to maintain her pace.

Sarah skirted the corner of the building she ran alongside and stopped. She took a moment to catch her breath, despite knowing better. She kneaded the knotted muscles in her legs, trying to ease the bite attacking them.

Sarah deflated against the building, tilted her head back, and looked at the darkening sky. Night loomed on the horizon, like a black shroud being pulled over the city. She needed to lay low and figure out what to do.

The tromping of the armed men rang in her ears. Their footfalls grew louder.

Sarah took a deep breath, then pushed off the wall. She trudged along the buildings, her pace slow and unsteady. Footfalls stalked her from behind. The sound of their gear shifting sent a wave of fear crashing into her. She peered over her shoulder.

Two armed men rushed after her. One had his rifle shouldered. The other had a pistol clutched between both of his hands. He lifted the pistol to get a bead on Sarah.

An opening within the drab building next to Sarah presented itself. The door was missing from its hinges. Darkness lurked within the interior.

A muffled voice called out, shouting at her back.

Sarah slipped inside the dimly lit structure–tripping over the sill. She stumbled, losing her footing. The ground rushed her, but she managed to balance herself out.

She kept moving, running into the gloom that filled the cavernous building. Each footfall echoed inside the hollow space. Sarah cringed, but moved just the same.

Dark, shadowy shapes populated the ground, spanning far and wide. What little she could see looked like machines or something similar.

The tromping of boots echoed all around her as the two men entered the structure.

She stayed low and moved through the building, trying to find a way out.

A set of lights sliced through the ether, catching Sarah's attention. The bright beams searched and scoured for their mark. The crackle of static lingered in the air, hinting at the armed men's position. A muffled voice fought the white noise sounding from the speaker.

The hiss of distortion nestled inside her ear as she hid behind a shelving unit. Cobwebs clung to the steel frame. The sticky web stuck to portions of her hair that brushed against it. Her hand swiped over the thick layer of dust that coated the sparse shelves.

Sarah ducked, then looked through the opening. Her face contorted in disgust. She ran her fingers through the matted strands of hair the cobwebs touched.

The beams of light split up, venturing to different points within the building.

Sarah gulped, then glanced around the building, trying to plot her way out. She spotted what might be a staircase at the far end of the shelving but struggled to tell for sure in the low light.

The henchmen drew closer to her position. The gleam from their flashlights washed over the ground near the shelves. She had to move.

Sarah crouched and worked her way down the length of the shelves to the end. She stayed silent–trying to conceal her location. The closer she got, the better look she had at the steel staircase that climbed the side of the wall.

It wound around the building, leading up to a second floor.

She moved around the railing to the landing, then up the winding stairs while trying to minimize her footfalls. Her feet clanged off each step–subtle but loud enough to disturb the silence.

A beam of light shone on her like a spotlight.

"She's heading upstairs," a gruff voice shouted.

Sarah charged up the steps in a mad dash. She hit the landing, then sprinted up the next set.

The lights below bounced and moved as the men gave pursuit. Through each gap between the steps, she caught a glimpse of the dark figures racing toward the landing.

One of the lights tilted to the floor, then blacked out. The other continued on.

Sarah shoved the door open at the top of the staircase, pushing it against the wall. She hit the landing and paused, looking down both stretches of long, dark hallway.

The tromping of boots against the steel steps made her flinch. She feared what the armed men would do to her if they caught up.

She bolted down the hallway to her right, running hard and fast.

The blinding darkness hampered her vision, making it a challenge to see where to go and what she might be heading into.

The rooms on either side of the hallway were consumed by the dark. Those with windows offered snippets of the ramshackle interiors.

Sarah dipped inside one of the offices, searching for a place to hide. The scant bit of light from the broken window on the far wall, cast the square room in deep shadows.

A tarp laid on the floor on the far side, the contents underneath concealed by the material.

The footfalls of her pursers creaked down the hallway.

Sarah turned to the open door. She had to hide and fast. The tarp was her best bet.

She scampered across the floor, her shoes shuffling through the debris. The sound made her cringe.

Dark Roads

The plastic crunched as she lifted the edge, blackness consumed the mass under the tarp.

Sarah dropped to her knees, then wormed her way under the crumpling material. It smelled old and stale, but still bearable. She laid on her back and allowed the tarp to rest on top of her.

The floor creaked.

Sarah placed her hand over her mouth to silence the fear that tried to escape. She missed her Glock 43. The world didn't seem as scary when she held the plastic grip of that gun in her hand.

"Bennet, what's your status, over?" a voice said, from the hallway near the office Sarah was hiding in. He crept closer. "Damn it. Where are you?" He sighed.

The creaking of the planks of wood under his weight signaled he was close.

Sarah pressed harder against her mouth.

The thumping of her heart pounded inside her head, making it seem louder. She couldn't penetrate the tarp's material to locate him.

The stench grew more stout the longer she stayed.

The man's footfalls trailed out of the room, leaving Sarah alone. She waited a few minutes before moving out from under the tarp.

Did he move on? Sarah thought.

The creaking boards faded with every second that passed.

Sarah tempted fate, poking her head out from under the tarp. No dark figures loomed in the shadows of the room, waiting for her to reveal herself.

The tarp crunched.

Sarah froze, listening for a response.

No heavy footfalls rushed her way, and no other sounds came to indicate trouble lurked close by.

She crawled out from under the cover, grateful to be free of the stench that assaulted her nose. The palms of her hands pressed to the dirty floor as she watched the hallway.

Sarah stood, then wiped her hands off on her filthy jeans. She searched for a weapon of any sort, then ran her hand over the floor, but couldn't spot or feel anything within the blackness.

Be quiet. Sarah thought, nearing the opened doorway.

She took a deep breath, then swallowed the fear that clogged her throat. Her pulse raced, heart hammering her chest without pause.

Sarah stayed close to the wall and crept along the sheetrock to the jamb. Her nerves bound tight from being hunted.

A lull of silence filled the hall except for the whistling of the wind exploiting any narrow cracks within the building.

Her shoulder pressed to the jamb as she rolled toward the corridor. She craned her neck and peered down the long, dark stretch of hallway that led back the way she came.

A figure moved within the shadows, then vanished from sight.

Sarah blinked, unable to tell if she had seen her pursuer, or if it had just been a figment of her strained imagination. She shook her head, clamped her lids shut, then looked again. Both stretches of corridor appeared to be clear.

She grabbed the jamb, holding firm as she stepped out into the hall. She gave a quick glance down the way she came while backing away. The creaking of the floor from the shadows signaled movement.

Sarah turned, then headed the opposite way, moving fast but also trying to minimize any noise. She skimmed over each office she passed, searching for another exit.

Dark Roads

"There has to be another way out of here," Sarah said, under her panicked breath. Her focus remained dead ahead, eyes probing for a way out.

The floor creaked behind Sarah.

The subtle sound chilled her blood. An eerie feeling of someone being close washed over her.

"Don't move," the familiar voice said, stern and direct. "Put your hands on the back of your head and turn–"

Another set of footfalls tromped down the hall from behind the armed man, fast and heavy.

"Bennet, where–what the–aw—"

The sharp report of gunfire rattled off from behind Sarah. The noise hammered her ears. She flinched and jumped from the flashes of orange muzzle fire.

The rounds punched the floor, then up the side of the wall to the ceiling. Fragments of the sheetrock rained down.

Sarah covered her head, then turned toward the intense strife.

Two black figures melded as one. Strained voices grew louder within the black mass. The shadowy figures slammed into the wall, creating a loud crescendo. A rifle clattered off the wooden floor. A flashlight mounted to the bottom flickered on, casting a wide gleam that blinded Sarah.

She shielded her face, bringing her hands up to block the light.

Grunts and growls filtered through panted breaths as the men duked it out. Their feet pounded the floor, hands grabbing at whatever they could on the other person's body.

The rifle was kicked. It spun about on the floor until the light shone on the feuding men.

Sarah caught a quick glimpse of Spencer's white ghost skull mask before he slammed into the wall, face first. His attacker hammered his kidneys, then threw a right cross at the back of his head.

Spencer side-stepped the blow.

The man's fist crashed into the wall. A painful wail fled his mouth as he stumbled back, cradling his hand.

Sarah backed away, then turned about face. She ran down the hall, her feet punishing the wood floor beneath her.

Her eyes adjusted some to the absence of light, allowing her to gauge the general outline of the walls and dead space of the rooms she passed.

She hooked the corner and continued running down the hall. Light at the end of the corridor shone through a window, catching her attention.

A single report echoed from the way she came, then silence. Soon, the victor would come for her.

The window had a thick film of grime that coated the glass, keeping Sarah from being able to see the outside world. She grabbed the bottom of the window and pulled up.

It didn't budge.

Sarah tried again. Her teeth gnashed, and her arms shook. The window broke loose.

The echo of boots hammering the floor rushed toward her down the corridor, giving ample incentive to get the window up.

The smell of the ocean filled her nose.

A cool breeze brushed over her flushed skin.

Sarah forced the window up until it stopped, then leaned out the opening. Her hands pressed against the windowsill. She looked down.

A dumpster sat near the base of the building, filled with black trash bags. She couldn't spot much of anything else within the hold.

Dark Roads

The pounding of feet grew louder. Faster. She had to get out now. She stared down at the bags below. There might be enough. No. The idea seemed outlandish. She'd likely break her leg, or neck.

The hammering of the man's bulk against the planks of wood drew closer.

"Sarah," Spencer said, shouting through the halls. "Don't run from me. You won't be safe on your own. I'm the only one who can protect you."

Sarah peered over her shoulder, unable to see the vile, disgusting man who stalked her through the dimness of the hallway. He'd become infatuated with her after their brief date that Mandy had sat up between them.

The dull light from the darkening sky stretched far down the hall before dwindling to nothing.

She took another look out of the window, then crawled over the windowsill. It didn't appear to be that far of a drop to the dumpster. She could make it.

The footfalls grew louder, clawing at her nerves.

Sarah dangled her legs from the window.

A single gulp of air filled her lungs.

She jumped.

The dumpster raced toward her. She hit the foul-smelling waste dead center. The bags tore open, leaking fluids on her hands and clothes.

The stench filled her nose and strangled her throat. A sticky substance clung to her hands. She swam through the discarded waste to the edge of the dumpster, then climbed over the edge.

Sarah dumped over to the ground, landing on her wobbling legs. She leaned against the side of the dumpster, gathering herself.

The burn of acid stung the back of her throat. She fought to keep what sparse particles of food that filled her stomach from erupting from her mouth. She gagged, but held firm.

Sarah pushed away from the trash bin, then glanced at the open window.

Spencer stood just beyond the opening, watching her every move. He hammered the windowsill with his fist and faded back into the ether, vanishing from Sarah's sight.

Dark Roads

CHAPTER FIVE

RUSSELL

Cathy removed her hand. She rotated her leg to the side to inspect the wound. "I'm fine. Just drive."

Max poked his head between the seats, licking at her face. His ears folded back onto his head. He whined, worried about his handler. She allowed him to comfort her with his kisses.

Russell diverted his gaze from the road to her thigh. He narrowed his eyes, trying to assess the damage. "I can't see for shit. Where the hell is the overhead light switch at?"

"Focus on driving. It doesn't look that bad. I think it just grazed me." Cathy leaned her head back against the headrest, then pressed her hand to the wound, covering it up. "If I keep pressure on it, it'll be all right for now. Besides, we need to put as much distance between us and those hillbillies as we can."

"Are you sure? It could be serious and not dressing it now could cause major problems." Russell searched the dash, trying to locate the headlights. A rounded knob touched the tips of his fingers near the door. He pulled.

The headlights came to life, casting a dull glow from the front of the truck. One side was brighter than the other, but it did the job.

Cathy rubbed under Max's chin, then made a kissy face at him. "I'm sure. This isn't the worst pain that I've ever experienced. It just stings some and aches. It's manageable."

Max leaned in closer, reaching for her face with his tongue.

"All right. That's enough. Sit back." Cathy kissed the side of the German shepherd's head, then pushed him away.

Max licked around his chops, then retreated to the backseat.

A weird smell sifted through the vents, followed by a hissing sound.

Russell trained his ear to the noise. "You hear that?"

Cathy took deep breaths, in and out, then said, "Hear what? I don't hear anything except for the wind howling."

The gauges on the dash didn't show any warnings or issues with the engine, but that meant little to nothing.

Russell rolled his window up, reducing the turbulence blasting through the opening. He held his finger in the air. "There. Do you hear that hissing sound?"

Cathy listened, then nodded. "Yeah. I hear it now. Are any of the gauges flashing on the dash?"

"No. Everything looks… wait a minute." The check engine light flickered, then dulled. Russell reached through the steering wheel, then wrapped his knuckles against the plastic covering. "The check engine light might be faulty. It's trying to light up, but it doesn't come on all the way."

Cathy craned her neck, then leaned to the side. "I'm not sure without taking a peek under the hood. Hopefully it's nothing too serious."

The thought of the Bronco dying didn't set well with Russell. They still had to stop off in Philly before he even thought of making it back home to his wife, Sarah, in Boston. He needed the Bronco to remain operational.

"We probably need to pull over and check out the engine to make sure it isn't too bad. If we press it and don't at least see what's wrong, we could make things worse. That, and we really need to address that gunshot wound on your thigh. I don't feel comfortable ignoring it."

Cathy checked her side-view mirror, then said, "I'm not so sure stopping right now would be good. You blew that guy's tire out, and Max gnawed on that scrawny guy's arm. Not to mention the sexual comments that creep made about me."

Russell understood Cathy's hesitation in stopping and the risk it imposed on them, but felt it prudent to check the engine out in a safe place.

"I understand, but I would rather us be able to pick a spot to hold up and address the engine and your leg versus the truck dying on the highway or your wound getting worse. At that point, we could be screwed. We both have too much at stake for that to happen," Russell replied. "I know we don't want to stop, but this is the right call."

The knocking sound grew louder, more intense the farther they drove. The check engine light burned a solid orange and stayed lit.

Cathy nodded her head. "All right. See if you can find a place off the main road here for us to stop. Maybe somewhere that isn't close to the highway incase those goons head down this way. I'd rather play it safe than sorry."

Dark Roads

They drove a bit longer, scouring the sides of the road for a place to hole up for a bit.

Russell pointed out of the windshield to the tall weeds growing alongside the shoulder. "There. Hold on." He slammed the brakes, bringing the Bronco to a skidding halt on the shoulder.

Cathy braced her free hand against the dash to keep her from being thrown forward. She peered out of the passenger side window to the gravel road next to the them.

There weren't any homes or businesses close by. It seemed worth checking out.

Russell pulled down the rocky slope and followed the road through the tall weeds that grew unchallenged. The tires dipped into the many pot holes that covered the makeshift path.

They drove farther away from the main road into the unknown.

The Bronco stuttered, then lunged forward. It got worse the longer it ran.

A line of trees lined the gravel road on Russell's side. Bushes and weeds filled any empty voids between the sprawling tree trunks.

Russell leaned close to the steering wheel, then squinted. "Is that a mailbox overgrown with weeds?"

Cathy stared in the same direction as Russell, then said, "Looks like it from here."

The dull lights of the Bronco shone over the thick blades and illuminated the head of the mailbox. A dirt drive came into view right after and sliced through the tree line.

Russell peered at the rich vegetation through the driver's side window, and spotted an older model home. "What do you think? It's pretty well concealed from the main road, but still close enough to I-66. Those trees and bushes block the house for the most part."

Cathy stared in the direction of the house, then down the long stretch of rocky road that faded off into darkness. "Well, it isn't the worst place I've ever stopped at. And, like you said, it's rather hidden. Do you think anyone lives there?"

The Bronco stopped shy of the dirt drive.

Russell shifted the clattering truck into park and eyed the house and the surrounding property. He couldn't spot any vehicles in front or on the sides of the rather grim looking home. "Can't say for sure without getting a closer look, but considering the overgrown grass and no vehicles parked in or around the house, I'm inclined to say no."

The engine hissed louder, acting as though it could die at any moment.

Cathy shifted her attention to the grumbling engine, then shook her head. "I guess we don't have much of a choice here."

"It'll be fine. Besides, don't you like being off grid?" Russell asked, smirking.

Cathy looked at him, then the eerie looking house. "Yeah, but not in the same house *The Texas Chainsaw Massacre* was filmed in."

"You won't have to worry about that," Russell replied, looking to the home.

"Why is that?" Cathy asked.

"That happened in Texas. We're in Virginia."

"Funny, Cage."

Russell shifted into drive and turned down the dirt driveway that led to the home.

Max peered out of the driver's side back seat window. His panting filled Russell's ears. The smell of beef jerky and other odd scents attacked Russell's nose, causing it to scrunch.

Dark Roads

The headlights cast their glow off the side of the house near the long, dirt drive. The paint had chipped away from the rotted siding, showing its age. It looked in dire shape from the outside.

Russell drove to the back of the house, searching for any vehicles or hints of life on the property.

A derelict garage sat about thirty feet or so from the home. The double doors were wide open. The interior of the structure was dark and void of any cars.

"Well, on the outset, it doesn't look like anyone's here," Cathy said.

Russell stopped, then placed the Bronco into park. He eyed the back of the house and the surrounding woods that lined the property. "Why don't you let me check out the house real quick? Just to be sure. I won't be long."

Cathy looked at the backseat. "Take Max with you. If anyone is inside the home or something isn't right, he'll let you know pretty fast."

"You sure?" Russell glanced to Max who sat in the middle of the bench seat, staring at them.

"Yeah. I'll be fine for a few minutes. If I spot any trouble or need anything, I'll hit the horn," Cathy replied, tilting her head.

Russell handed her his Glock. "Here."

"Don't you need that?"

Russell shook his head. "I took John Deere's from the station. Besides, I'll have Max with me. I'd feel more at ease if you had something to defend yourself with."

Cathy took the Glock 17 from Russell, and set it in her lap. "Don't take your sweet time, all right?"

"I don't think you're going to have to worry about that." Russell looked to Max, then said, "You ready, big man?"

Max groaned, then stood. He moved toward the back driver's side door and barked.

Russell tossed open his door, then stepped out.

Cathy cleared her throat. "Watch yourself in there."

"We will." Russell shut his door, then turned to the back seat of the SUV.

The anxious German shepherd groaned, then barked. He pawed at the window as Russell opened the door.

"Come on. Let's check things out."

Max bolted from the back seat in a blink and hit the ground running—his nose trained to the dirt, tail wagging. He paused, then lifted his front paw. His ears twitched, gaze looking to the open field behind the garage.

"What is it?" Russell asked, searching for whatever had captured the German shepherd's attention.

The open field showed no shadowy figures scampering about. Silence loomed large except for the hoots from owls that resided in the nearby trees.

Max lowered his leg and dropped his head back to the ground, investigating the unfamiliar surroundings.

"Keep your eyes and ears open for any trouble." Russell made his way toward the screened in porch with John Deere's piece clutched in his palm. He cycled a round, skimming through the torn screen that enclosed the porch.

Max followed at his side, sniffing the ground as they moved through the weeds.

A concrete walkway led from the back of the worn, wooden steps of the house to the garage. Grass grew through the fissures that snaked along the surface.

In the middle of the yard, just off the beaten path of the walkway, was an old-fashioned well with a hand pump. Russell wondered if it worked.

Dark Roads

Max trotted up the walkway, stopping shy of the steps. He groaned, then pawed at the corner of the rotting wood door.

Russell trailed behind, flanking the anxious canine who had his nose near the edge of the entrance.

Cathy was right about the unsettling vibe the home gave off.

Max didn't bark or show any signs of hesitation. He waited patiently for the door to open. Max looked up to Russell.

"Yeah. Yeah."

Russell cracked open the door.

The hinges squeaked loud in the dull silence.

Max forced his way through the opening and onto the porch.

Russell pulled the door open wider, then climbed the wooden steps. His hand closed over the grip of the pistol a hair tighter–his nerves tightening a notch more.

The patio was open and free of clutter.

A carpet of leaves crunched under his boots.

Max patrolled the width of the space, trotting to the far wall then back to Russell's side. He sniffed around the base of the walls, then planted himself right in front of the back door leading into the home itself.

Russell leaned in close, peering through the grime that coated the glass to the lingering darkness of the home.

The kitchen appeared empty with no furnishings in the drab space. The vague outline of cabinets lined the far wall with no appliances fixed in the black open spaces between the counters.

Russell felt his back pocket, then slipped his fingers inside the opening. He pulled his phone out and thumbed the power button.

The screen splashed the manufacturer logo, then booted up.

Russell waited for the phone to come online.

Max grew impatient, pawing at the jamb, then the base of the door.

45

"All right, I'm working on it. I can't see as well as you in the dark, so give me a second."

The phone was at ten percent.

Russell turned on the flashlight.

A bright light shone from the back of his phone, illuminating the worn and faded paint of the door's surface.

Here we go.

He grabbed the knob, then turned.

The gears inside clicked.

Russell pulled on the knob, but the door wouldn't budge. He tugged a bit harder, jerking toward him.

The door broke free of the jamb.

Max darted inside.

"Max, wait up, will ya?" Russell said, in a loud whisper.

Max ignored the command and sniffed around the kitchen.

Russell slipped through the back door, and shined his flashlight over the abandoned house. The wooden floor creaked under his weight.

A musty, earthy smell made Russell's nose crinkle. The scent reminded him of rotting wood or wet socks that had been tossed in a hamper and left.

The wall paper had lost its adhesion and peeled away from the walls in places. Cobwebs clung to the corners and nooks. The silky webs were coated in dust, and whatever insects dared cross the tangled webs.

Max trotted past Russell, heading for the hallway that led toward the front of the house.

Russell strode across the kitchen to the window above the sink. He peered out of the unkempt glass at the open field.

Bark!

Max.

46

Dark Roads

Russell backed away from the counter, then turned on his heels to face the hallway. He made a beeline to the opening, and brought his piece to bear.

"Max? Where are you?" Russell walked down the dark, narrow passage.

Bark.

Russell followed the sharp barks and nails scratching. A black void loomed next to him from the opened door that led to the basement. Russell shinned his light over the ether, illuminating the stairs that descended into the depths of the unknown.

He continued on, making his way around the banister.

Max faced the far wall that led into a massive living space. He clawed at the baseboards; his nose trained to the dusty cobwebs that stuck to the walls.

"What did you find?"

Russell shone the light on the wall where Max pawed.

He groaned, then jumped back.

A mouse ran alongside the baseboards, then skirted the corner of the wall.

Russell jumped back. He hated the small vermin.

Christ.

"Leave that filthy thing alone, and let's check out the remainder of the house."

Max peered around the corner of the wall, but didn't give chase to the tiny varmint that infested the home.

They cleared the remainder of the bottom and top floor, finding nothing more than dust, cobwebs, and some furniture within the entire place.

Russell made his way down the rickety staircase and the dark hallway to the kitchen. He closed the door to the basement for added security and his own peace of mind. The thought of a rat coming into the home made his skin crawl.

Max ran out of the back door, over the porch, and into the weeds.

Russell tucked the piece inside his waistband and made his way back to the Bronco.

Cathy had her door slung open, petting the crown of Max's head.

"Well?" she asked.

"It's clear, minus the bugs and rodents," Russell answered, looking at the abandoned home. "Doesn't look like anyone's been here for some time."

Max licked Cathy's hand, then backed away, giving her room to get out of the Bronco.

"That's good. If we can find a flashlight, then I'll take a look at the engine to see what's wrong." Cathy grabbed the edge of the door and maneuvered her legs out. The shadows hid her face. The discomfort festering in her thigh was evident by the subtle grunts and slow movements she made.

Russell offered her his hand, helping her out of the truck. "I thought we'd check it out in the morning at first light."

"Are you talking about staying here for the night?" Cathy lowered her leg to the ground, then leaned back against the Bronco.

"Yeah. I know it's not ideal, but you're hurt, we're beyond exhausted, and with it being night, it's going to be too difficult to check out the engine without a good source of light. The Bronco's pretty much out of sight from the road I think, so we should be good."

Cathy shrugged, then pushed away from the truck, favoring her uninjured leg. "Damn it. All right. I hate to waste the time, but you're right."

48

"Just go inside with Max. I'll gather our supplies and be in shortly." Russell shut the door, then turned to face Cathy.

"You sure? I'm not completely helpless right now, Cage." Cathy pointed at the interior of the truck. "I don't need my leg to carry anything. I can help."

Russell held his hands up in protest. "I didn't mean to imply you couldn't. I just want you to rest, and take it easy is all. This won't take but a few minutes."

Cathy shrugged. "All right. I'll see you inside, then. Come on, boy."

Max snapped too and followed his handler. Cathy limped past the well pump toward the porch.

Russell walked around the front of the Bronco and retrieved the keys from the ignition. He gathered the supplies from the floorboard and slammed the driver's side door.

He checked the remainder of the Bronco for anything of use. The vehicle belonged to Marcus Wright, the low life who had kidnapped Cathy and held her hostage at one of his lumber mills.

In the far back seat, Russell found a blanket and a bag. He grabbed both and closed the rear hatch.

Russell faced the dark, abandoned house, then muttered, "Home sweet home."

Derek Shupert

CHAPTER SIX

SARAH

Her ankle throbbed, pulsating with pain. The longer Sarah walked, the more intense the discomfort grew. She braced her hand against the rigid surface of the brick building she trudged alongside, trying to relieve the pressure from her foot.

The leap from the window to the trash bin was a bold move—one Sarah never thought she'd do in a million years—but armed men and the Creeper had pushed her over the edge and into that steel container of filth.

Sarah peered over her shoulder, panting and searching for Spencer or the armed men, but the coming night dulled the daylight–making it harder to see. She spotted no figures lurking in the dark corners of the buildings close by or the vehicles that sat on the sides of the street.

Damn it.

The smell lingering from her body paled in comparison to the pain that tormented her ankle. Sarah twisted her leg to the side, then dipped her chin. She pulled her grungy pant leg up to examine the damage. The absence of any light and her shoe hampered her vision.

Sarah lowered her pant leg, then looked over the desolate street and buildings. Not a single soul lurked on the far sidewalk or near the sprawling structures.

The surroundings didn't look familiar, especially in the dark. She didn't frequent this part of Boston often, if ever, so she was at a loss as to where to go.

Sarah pushed off the wall and limped down the sidewalk. The exterior of the building acted like a crutch. Barking dogs and gunfire crackling in the sky randomly made her flinch. She skimmed over the darkening streets and buildings, watching for any unscrupulous thugs looking for an easy target.

A car drove past her, heading toward the intersection up head. The bright red glow of the taillights flashed as the sedan slowed, then continued on through the intersection. It sped away as Sarah turned the corner.

She hobbled down the sidewalk, drawing her arms across her chest. Her clothes clung to skin–wet with sweat and whatever ungodly fluids had spilled from the trash. The wind brushed over her exposed skin, making her shiver. She pulled her arms tighter.

The constant threat of being chased kept her body tense, and her guard up.

Sarah needed a moment to sit and process everything, but where?

A ghastly gray figure emerged from the alley she passed. His sudden appearance snatched her breath and made her hobble backward.

Dark Roads

She lifted her arms, then balled her hands into fists—a gut reaction to the ominous-looking figure who stood before her like death itself.

The hood of his jacket draped over his head, cloaking his face. The stench grew tenfold, adding to the already foul smell that lingered from her own battered frame.

"Don't come near me," Sarah said, her voice low and timid. "Stay away from me."

A car backfired up the street.

Sarah recoiled, looking away from the figure before her.

The man grabbed her arm, yanking her toward the abysmal gloom of the dark alleyway.

"Let me go." Sarah jerked her arm back, but couldn't rip it away from the man's hand.

Her body thrashed, and her legs kicked. The injured ankle gave, causing Sarah to lose her balance and stumble.

The cloaked man dragged her farther into the blackness, away from any prying eyes that could see the sinister act he had in store for her.

Sarah fell to the concrete.

Her knees hit the pavement, scraping the skin.

She fell forward, then over to her side.

"Help," she said, screaming at the top of her lungs.

The man stopped, then stooped down. He held a blade at her throat, the sharp edge pressed against her skin. "Scream one more time, and I'll open you up."

Sarah shuddered, fighting the urge to scream. She clenched her jaw and held her tongue.

The man towed her a bit farther, then discarded her next to a pile of trash bags.

He towered over her, offering no demands of any sort.

Sarah kicked her legs, searching for that sweet spot between his hips.

The man knocked her feeble attempts to the side, then mounted her. His bulk rested on her thighs, keeping her legs from moving. Her balled fists punched at his face, or any other part of his body she could strike.

"No. No. Get off me." Sarah caught a lucky blow, hitting him square on the chin.

He paused, then rubbed his jaw. "Oh, I'm going to enjoy this."

Sarah swung at his head again, hoping to catch him with another lucky strike. She lifted her hips into the air and moved her legs, trying to wiggle them free.

A heavy hand smashed into the side of Sarah's face. Her jaw ached from the glancing blow.

The man leaned forward, placing the blade back against her throat. "You shouldn't have done that." His warm, fetid breath hit the side of her face, adding insult to injury.

Sarah pressed the palms of her hands to his chest and pushed, but the man's weight was too much for her to move.

He kissed the side of her neck, his tongue slithering over her flesh like a snake. The coarse, wiry strands of hair from his beard grated on her skin. Her flesh crawled with disgust.

His free hand explored her body. Lying there, at the man's mercy, Sarah wondered if this was how it would end—her being raped then murdered in an alley like some piece of trash.

Tears formed in her eyes. A whimper of sadness fled her trembling lips as she pushed on the man's chest.

A light shone from the direction of the street. It grew brighter and headed their way. The black-clad figure taking advantage of Sarah hadn't noticed it.

"Hey, get off of her," the stern, feminine voice said.

Dark Roads

The man pulled away from Sarah's neck and sat up straight. His hand left her breast, then pointed at the stranger standing off to the side of them. "If you know what's good for you, then you'll–"

The woman struck the man in the head with her bag, knocking him off balance. He pulled the knife away from Sarah's throat, then leaned to the side. He stood off her legs, giving her room to move.

The black-clad figure straddled her legs, then pointed the tip of his knife at the woman.

Sarah kicked him in the balls, ripping a painful scream from the man's mouth.

He dropped the blade to the concrete, then dumped over to his side.

The woman offered Sarah her hand, then helped her off the dirty pavement. "Are you ok?"

"Better now, no thanks to this piece of crap." Sarah got to her feet, favoring her pulsating ankle.

The man writhed on the concrete, balled into the fetal position and cupping his genitals. He groaned and panted, trying to catch his breath. "You damn–bitch."

The light from the woman's phone shone over the man's knife on the ground and the smirched, nasty rags he wore. The meager blade caught Sarah's attention. She bent down and retrieved the weapon from the pavement.

The woman placed her hand on Sarah's shoulder, then said, "Come on. Let's go while we can."

Sarah contemplated using the knife on the vile thug. Perhaps she'd do the world a favor and castrate him–take the other weapon from between his legs, so he couldn't use it on anyone else.

The notion fell by the wayside, though, as killing an unarmed man didn't set well with her now that she had the upper hand.

She pointed the tip of the blade at the man. "You're lucky I don't take your beans and frank, you sick piece of shit. Consider this you winning the lottery."

"Come on." The woman tugged on her arm, pulling her away from the whimpering man.

Sarah pocketed the knife, then turned away. She placed her hand on the woman's arm. "Thank you for your help."

The woman's face was cast in shadows, offering only the outline of her angular cheekbones and other subtle features the darkness tried to hide.

The flashlight from her phone shone at the ground in front of them, lighting their way out of the alley to the sidewalk. "No thanks needed. I'm just glad I passed by when I did. This can be a rough neighborhood, even with the power on and everything not out of control like it is."

"Seems like most of Boston is rough right now." Sarah removed her hand, then tried to stand on her own. The pain in her ankle hurt, causing her to lift her leg from the ground and favor it. The plummet to the dumpster from the window must have hurt her ankle when she hit. She didn't recall hitting anything within the trash-filled container that would've hurt her leg, but then again, it happened so fast she might not have noticed doing so. "Damn it."

The woman held out her arms, grabbing her by the waist. "Here. My apartment is up the street. Why don't you come with me, and we'll take a look at it."

Sarah could manage on her own and didn't want to drag anyone else into her chaotic world. "I appreciate the offer, but I'll be fine. It's not that bad. I probably just tweaked it when that guy attacked me."

The woman shook her head. "It looks bad enough that you're limping. Come on. I'm not taking no for an answer. Besides, staying out here with lowlife's like that guy back there won't do you any good. I insist."

"I really don't want to be a bother," Sarah said, limping alongside the younger, smaller woman.

"You're not. I couldn't live with myself if I left you out here after experiencing what you did and being hurt as well. It wouldn't be right," the woman replied, taking Sarah's arm and putting it over her shoulders to hold her weight. "From the looks of it, you could use a moment to rest."

You have no idea.

Derek Shupert

CHAPTER SEVEN

RUSSELL

The torrid wind exploited any imperfections within the siding of the exterior walls. A subtle whistling echoed throughout the hollow space. Branches slapped against the house, adding to the other odd noises that lingered in the abandoned home.

Max didn't care for the unwanted sounds, growling from his core as he searched for the source.

"It's ok, boy," Cathy said, petting the crown of his head from the flat of her back. "Just the weather outside being unruly is all. Nothing you haven't heard before."

The German shepherd leaned into her hand, soaking up the attention like a sponge. His head lay on the floor at her side, the perfect watchman for the night.

"How's the leg feeling?" Russell asked, standing behind Max and Cathy at the boarded-up window in the living room.

"It's doing all right. Still throbs and aches, but the bleeding has lessened, I think." Cathy shifted her weight, trying to get comfortable on the wafer-thin cushions they robbed from the broken-down couch that sat at an angle in the far corner of the room. "Pretty lucky you finding that go bag and blanket in the back of the Bronco."

Russell peered through the narrow gaps between the boards, skimming over the front yard and the gravel road that ran in front of the property. "Seems like Marcus Wright's goons liked to be prepared. Good for us in the end."

The living room of the abandoned house had become their sanctuary for the night. A less than desirable place, given its dire state of repair, but it had a roof and four walls.

"True. The blanket is a nice touch, so are the medical supplies, rope, and flashlight." Cathy slapped the black metal casing of the Maglite against her hand. "I just wish this damn flashlight would work a bit better. I think the batteries are shot. That light should be a lot brighter than it is."

Light flickered from the bezel, then faded away.

Russell nodded, then scratched at the festering itch on the side of his scruffy face. "Have you eaten anything yet?"

He stepped away from the window and walked over to them.

Cathy ran her fingers over the mound of sweets. "I had a Snickers. That's about it. I'm leaving the jerky for Max, if that's ok? Kind of hard to see what all is here with it being so dark and all."

Russell bent down, then ran his fingers along Max's spine. "Yeah. I'd planned on giving him the jerky. I'll nibble on what's left."

Max tilted his head back, looking up at Russell. A yawn attacked him, his maw opening wide.

"Well, there should be plenty here." Cathy grabbed a handful of the sugary foods. "I try not to eat too much candy. It normally doesn't agree with me."

"I think I grabbed some salted nuts as well. Can't remember." Russell dipped his chin and searched the floor for the flashlight, wanting to see if he could get it working.

"Haven't found any nuts other than the ones coated in chocolate," Cathy replied, shifting her weight.

Russell felt around the floor, finding the flashlight next to Cathy. "How's the pain?"

Cathy groused, then said, "In my leg or the knot forming in my back?"

"I told you they had some weird kind of couch thing in one of the upstairs rooms. I can haul it down here. Won't be a problem." Russell slapped the flashlight against his hand, then thumbed the switch on the side. The light flickered, then died.

"You're in no condition to be shuffling furniture around, especially from the second floor and down those rickety looking stairs," Cathy said. "Without having this gunshot on the side of my thigh, you're just about in as bad of shape as I am. Both of us can't be out of commission."

Russell took apart the Maglite, then slipped the batteries out. He blew inside the housing. "I'm not dying or feeble. If it'll help make you a bit more comfortable, I don't mind doing it. I know those cushions we pulled from the couch over there don't give much cushion between you and the floor."

Cathy tried to turn to face Russell, but grimaced in pain. "You've never camped before, have you, Cage? Roughed it outside with nothing but the ground God provided and a blanket of stars to fill your eyes before drifting off to sleep?"

"I think we've established that I'm rather lacking in outdoor survival training." Russell slammed the batteries back into the Maglite, then screwed the top back on. He thumbed the button.

"It's a waste of time messing with that damn thing." Cathy lifted her head from the blanket, then probed around the wound with her fingers. "I'd just leave it be. There's no telling how long they had it in that bag or how old those batteries are."

Russell stood with the Maglite clutched in his hand. "I'm going to check the Bronco to see if maybe they have any batteries that I overlooked. I'll be right back."

"Do you want Max to go with you?" Cathy asked, her tone unsteady.

"No. I'm good, unless he needs to use the bathroom or something," Russell answered. Max didn't budge from the floor or look too keen on moving from his spot next to Cathy. "He doesn't look like he wants to venture outside right now. If he needs to go, he can find a spot to do his business somewhere inside. I doubt the house will mind. It wouldn't be the worst thing to happen in here, I imagine. I'll be right back."

Russell turned and walked away, heading out of the living room into the foyer. He passed the staircase, then dug his hand into the front pocket of his pants.

The tiny bottle of Jack Daniels he'd snagged from the convenience store weighed on his mind. His aligning body needed a fix to curb the subtle pain. A quick fix to help him through the long journey ahead.

He glanced over his shoulder, looking back at Cathy, acting as if he'd done something wrong. He'd grown used to such habits with Sarah.

Just a taste. Enough to take the edge off and dull the pain. Nothing more.

Dark Roads

The little bottle was the closest thing he had to pain killers. It'd have to do in a pinch.

Russell stopped, then drifted back into the ether of the narrow walkway that ran beside the staircase. He leaned back against the wall, unscrewing the cap from the bottle.

The rich scent of the whiskey filled his nose–a mixture of bananas, honey, and wood.

His mouth watered from excitement.

A single drink, nay a sip, is all he sought.

The rim of the bottle pressed to his lips.

Russell tilted his head back, taking a gulp of the spirit.

The flavorful whiskey splashed over his tongue, then down his throat. It coursed through his body, dumping into the depths of his stomach.

The liquor warmed and relaxed his body, putting Russell into a state of momentary peace. He licked his lips, removing the evidence, and took another swig.

A crashing sound from the second floor snared his attention from the stolen moment with the bottle. He removed the opening from his lips, screwed the cap back on, then shoved the tiny bottle back into his pocket.

Max barked from the living room.

"Russell, are you ok?" Cathy asked in a raised voice.

"Yeah. I'm fine. That wasn't me." Russell moved around the stairs, stopping on the landing and glancing up to the second floor.

"You don't think someone is up there, do you?"

"There shouldn't be. Max and I checked over the house before you came in. We didn't see or find any signs of anyone staying here."

"It could be a raccoon or something."

"Yeah. That's probably what it is, but I'm going to go check it out regardless." Russell pulled his piece from the waistband of his jeans and walked toward the stairs.

Max trotted across the living room to the foyer. He looked at Russell, his body taut and ears standing on end.

"You coming with me?"

The German shepherd galloped up the stairs and past Russell to the second floor.

Russell scaled the staircase, one rickety step at a time.

Max waited for him at the landing, his head pointed at the dark walkway that ran next to the railing.

It's got to be an animal, Russell thought. Given the dire state of the home, it'd be easy for a squirrel or raccoon to find a way inside through the many holes in the walls and ceiling.

Russell craned his neck, peering through the railing at the dark rooms that lined the far wall. He hit the landing, then stopped. He roved his pistol and slipped his finger through the trigger guard.

Max took the lead, sniffing the floor and heading toward the bedrooms. He paused, then stared dead ahead. His dark coat blended with the darkness, offering only the vague hint of his large frame.

The floor creaked under their weight. The hissing of wind through the fissures in the walls added to the unsettling ambiance of the house. Russell gulped, sweeping the corridor from side to side. A rustling noise sounded from behind the closed door to his right.

Max charged the bedroom, then lowered his head. He pawed at the base, sniffing and groaning.

"What do you think? Is it a racoon, squirrel, or a giant-sized rat?"

Max clawed at the bottom of the door, fighting to get inside.

Russell flanked the German shepherd. He listened, training his ear to the ruckus. "Max, shush."

Dark Roads

The canine refused to give up his campaign, clawing at the wood that splintered and cracked from the bottom of the door.

"Seriously. Stop, will ya?" Russell scooted Max away, pushing him to the side of the entrance with his leg. "Just hold on for a second and let me listen without you shredding the door."

The banging noise remained, but he couldn't hear any other movement. Russell grabbed the doorknob, twisted it counterclockwise, then pushed forward.

The hinges creaked as loud as the aged floor they stood on. The door swung open, and the unholy stench of fecal matter and mildew escaped from the enclosed space.

Russell coughed, then covered his mouth and nose.

Max stood at his side, peering through the narrow opening at the dark and grim-looking space. He took a step forward, testing the air with his nose. A growl loomed from his throat, but Russell couldn't find the cause of his angst.

"I can't see for crap," Russell said, under his breath, fighting to pierce the ether before him. He blinked, rubbed his eyes, then opened them wide. It did little good.

Damn it.

Max trotted in, inspecting the bedroom.

Russell followed, pushing the door open farther. His hand remained fixed to his face, eyes trying to get a feel for the layout of the bedroom. He hadn't stepped inside the room earlier when he did a quick sweep of the floor.

Gaping holes filled with hollow blackness dotted the walls. A mattress frame rested against the far wall.

Max sniffed at the floor, then took a step back. He shook his head.

The crunch of glass sounded under Russell's boots. He glanced down at the floor and squinted, spotting what looked to be a large picture or painting that had fallen from the wall.

Max growled, snaring Russell's attention.

A loud bang made him flinch. His heart skipped a beat, and his pulse spiked.

What the hell was that?

The canine faced the closet door, baring his fangs and lowering to the floor.

The wind howled, low and dull one minute, then louder the next. The closet door moved on its own, swaying back and forth. It slammed against the jamb, then opened again.

Max inched his way toward the closet, stalking whatever lurked on the other side. The stout stench grew the closer they got.

Russell trained his gun at the closet, then stepped around Max. The blinding darkness within the enclosed space made it impossible to see what might be inside. He reached for the flailing door and grabbed the doorknob.

Max growled louder, more intense than before. He probed the air, then barked.

A scratching noise sounded from inside, then rustling.

Russell took a deep breath and yanked the door open.

A shadowy figure sat in the void, resting on a stack of boxes about waist high. It looked like an animal from its size. The creature growled, then vanished back into the blackness beyond the wall.

Max lunged forward, barking at the animal.

Russell sighed, then bent over. "It's ok, Max. It's just a damn raccoon."

Max sniffed the inside of the closet, then rose on his hind legs. His front paws rested on the animal's nest, barking at the black void within the wall.

"It's probably long gone now," Russell said, batting the air in front of his face. "Probably got in through a hole in the roof and made this room his pad, or his toilet."

Russell grabbed the anxious German shepherd by the collar and pulled him away.

The large canine resisted, barking at the opening without pause.

"Come on, Max. Stop it. Let's get out of here. Does that smell not bother you?" Russell asked, ready to leave the creature's stomping grounds.

Max backed away from the closet, then dropped to his front paws.

Russell turned and headed for the hallway, wanting to get away from the smell of the animal's droppings fast.

"Now, Max."

Max gave his coat a good shake, then trotted past Russell to the hallway.

Russell closed the door behind them, leaving the animal to roam about within its dwelling. He made his way around the railing to the landing.

The smell embedded inside his nose, refusing to let up. Russell ran his fingers under both nostrils, then blew, trying to expel the foul stench.

He stayed close to the wall and worked his way down the staircase. Max raced to the bottom, then vanished into the living room.

Russell hit the landing, thankful to be far away from the animal's droppings. "Damn raccoon mulling about inside a bedroom. The room upstairs smelt like a toilet."

Cathy didn't respond.

He hit the landing at the base of the stairs, then peered into the living room.

Max sat on his haunches at her side, standing watch over his slumbering handler.

"Keep an eye on her. I'll be right back."

The German shepherd shifted his weight between his front legs, but stayed put.

Russell walked around the banister and down the hallway toward to the kitchen. He yawned, cupping his mouth with his hand. His eyes watered.

The door leading out of the screened in porch slapped the jamb, battering the frail wooden door.

The howling wind tore through the mesh covering, kicking up the leaves in a cyclone of dead debris that blew everywhere.

Russell pushed his way through the clattering door and over to the Bronco. Each step drained him. A solid night of sleep beckoned him from the interior of the abandoned house.

The pistol remained fixed in his grasp, held firm as he surveyed the surrounding plot of land that encompassed the property. No shadowy figures lurked through the blackness, easing his tired mind.

The Bronco's interior light illuminated the worn seats of the truck. Russell leaned through the driver's side, tossed his pistol onto the dusty dash, and hunted for the batteries.

Russell searched under the seats and any other compartment for any spare batteries, but found none. He did find the portable power bank wedged between the passenger seat and the center console. It must have gotten separated from the other items taken from the convenience store.

The wind pressed against the passenger side door, slamming into his body–shoving him forward. Russell pushed the door open, then wedged his backside against it. He fiddled with the plastic

Dark Roads

casing that housed the power bank, trying to tear through the material. He placed the corner of the package inside his mouth and ripped it apart.

The power bank dropped out of the packaging and into the passenger seat. Russell sifted through the handful of parts included and found a 12-volt car adapter. Perfect.

Russell dug it out of the packaging along with the short, orange charging cable. He removed the cigarette lighter from the housing and shoved the small, white adapter in its place. The charging cable plugged into the open port on the front.

A green light lit up from the top of the adapter. Russell smiled, glad that his phone would soon be charged. He retrieved the power bank from the seat and connected it to the charging cable. Four bright-white lights flashed on the side, then blinked.

The interior light died, casting the Bronco into darkness. Russell tossed the empty packaging to the backseat, retrieved his piece from the dash, then stepped away from the truck.

The wind slammed the door shut.

Russell pulled his hands away. He stowed the pistol in the waistband of his jeans, then made for the house.

The screen door continued to slap the jamb, creating a boisterous, annoying sound that grated on his nerves.

Russell secured the door with the latch mounted on the wall, hoping that would fix the problem. He walked through the back door and twisted the rusted deadbolt clockwise, locking it.

Another big yawn overtook Russell, making his eyes water even more. They stung this time and ached. He needed sleep, stat.

The floor in the hallway creaked from his weight.

A sharp bark and growl sounded from the living room.

"It's just me, Max."

Russell skirted the banister and entered the living room.

Max laid at Cathy's side with his head fixed in the direction of the foyer.

Cathy didn't respond to his presence, slumbering on the floor in a deep sleep. A slight whistle escaped her mouth.

Russell dropped to the floor next to Max, then rolled to his back. The German shepherd sniffed, then licked his hand. Russell rubbed under his maw and stared at the cracked ceiling.

He thought of Sarah and her sweet, warm smile as he drifted off to sleep.

Dark Roads

CHAPTER EIGHT

SARAH

The flight of stairs leading to the woman's third floor apartment challenged Sarah's aching ankle. Each step tormented the throbbing joint–making Sarah wince.

"When we get inside, we'll need to get your leg elevated. That should help to reduce any swelling." The woman stayed at her side, helping Sarah up the mountain of steps.

Sarah slid her hand along the banister, hobbling up each precarious step one at a time.

"I do really appreciate your kindness," Sarah said, through strained breath. "It has been a rough couple of days for sure."

They hit the landing and stopped.

The woman took a deep breath, then said, "It's no problem, really. My apartment is just down the hall here, fourth door on the right."

Dark Roads

The flashlight from the back of her phone shone down the length of the dark corridor. It penetrated the ether only so far before fading off.

Sarah turned, then peered over the railing to the bottom floor. The Creeper lingered in her thoughts, keeping Sarah on edge and looking over her shoulder.

The woman placed her hand on her arm. "Don't worry, honey. That bad man isn't there. You're safe."

Safe? Hardly.

"Yeah." Sarah limped away from the railing, then made her way down the hall with the woman at her side.

A door slammed from the way they came. She flinched, then peered over her shoulder to a shadowy figure heading for the stairs. Their footsteps echoed down the dark, enclosed corridor. She scanned over the closed doors they passed. Sarah wondered who dwelled within the apartment and more so, if they aimed to hurt her.

"Right here." The woman dug her hand into the depths of the large purse she toted on her shoulder. "I hate having this bag at times. Trying to fish my keys out can be a real chore."

She trained the light from her phone on the purse while her hand sifted through the contents inside.

The door rattled against the jamb. The deadbolt clinked.

The woman paused, then glanced up to the cracked door. "Hannah, what have I told you about opening the door like that?"

The door opened farther, revealing a young, red-headed girl staring back at them. She looked to be six years old, or around there, from what Sarah could tell.

"I'm sorry, Mommy. I was waiting for you to get back. When I looked through the peephole, I saw it was you," Hannah replied in a soft, tender tone. "I only wanted to help."

The young girl opened the door farther, standing with her brown teddy bear clutched in her arms. She looked at her mom, then Sarah with large, sad eyes.

The woman switched off the flashlight on her phone, then shoved it into her purse. "It's ok, sweetie, but I wish you listened better. From now on, you don't open this door for any reason unless I say otherwise, ok?"

Hannah nodded. "Yes, Mommy." She vanished behind the door.

"My daughter. She can be a handful at times. Listening and following instructions aren't her strong suit. I normally don't leave her here alone like this, but I had to run out to get supplies and medicine and didn't want to take her out into that mess." The woman pressed against the door and pushed. She sighed. "Move the chair, please."

A loud scraping noise sounded from the apartment.

Sarah braced her hand against the jamb. "I can understand that. The lawlessness out there is concerning for sure, and not to be taken lightly."

The door swung open without restriction.

The woman helped Sarah inside her small apartment. She dropped her purse to the tile floor. It hit with a dense thud. "Can you get the door for me, Hannah?"

"Sure thing, Mommy."

Hannah closed the door, then engaged the deadbolt.

"We'll get you situated on the couch here," the woman said.

Sarah limped around the worn, brown, leather rocking chair and coffee table to the couch. She turned and plopped down on the meager cushions that had little to no fluff. The springs creaked and popped.

"Let's get that leg elevated." The woman grabbed a pillow from the rocking chair.

Dark Roads

"Is it ok if I rest my foot on the coffee table?" Sarah asked.

The woman dismissed the question with a flick of her wrist. "Go right ahead. This old thing is so beat up I don't really care anymore. I need to replace it at some point." She tucked a pillow under Sarah's foot.

Hannah stood near the kitchen on the far side of the room, cast in shadows. The few large candles lit within the apartment offered a bit of reprieve from the darkness. "Is she ok?"

"Yes. I think Mrs.–" The woman paused, then placed her hands on her hips. She shook her head, then extended her hand. "I'm sorry. I didn't catch your name. I'm Tiffany."

Sarah leaned forward and shook it. "Sarah."

Tiffany turned, then pointed at the young girl. "That's Hannah, the apple of my eye."

Sarah waved at her, offering a warm smile through the tiredness and discomfort stabbing at her ankle. "Nice to meet you."

Hannah hugged her bear a bit tighter, then swayed from side to side. She hesitated for a moment, then waved back.

"All right. Let's take a look at that ankle, shall we?"

Tiffany grabbed the bottom of Sarah's pants and pulled it up some. She placed her palm flat on the coffee table and leaned closer. "Hannah, grab my phone from my purse and bring it here, please. I guess I need to see about getting more candles or something. It's still pretty dark in here."

"Okay, Mommy." Hannah held tight onto her teddy bear and walked to her mother's purse on the floor.

"Does it hurt if you bend your foot or rotate it?" Tiffany asked.

Sarah moved her foot in a circle, then back and forth. Her face contorted in discomfort. "It hurts when I do it, but I can."

75

Hannah walked up behind Tiffany, and handed her the phone.

"Thanks, baby girl." Tiffany thumbed the flashlight on, then trained the beam at Sarah's foot. She pulled the dingy sock down and took a closer look. "Yeah. It's swollen. Probably just a sprain, though."

Sarah craned her neck, trying to see the extent of the damage. The skin around her ankle puffed out some, but it didn't look too bad from what she could see.

Hannah hid behind her mom, poking her head out to the side and looking at Sarah's ankle. "Does it hurt real bad? I've hurt my knee before. Mommy had to clean it off and it stung a lot."

"Not too bad, sweetie. It'll be fine in no time." Sarah smiled at the shy, timid girl who clung to the teddy bear like a lifeline.

Hannah reminded Sarah of Jess, her daughter. She missed that age of innocence and purity.

"I would say putting some ice on it would help, but with the power out, I don't have any." Tiffany thumbed the flashlight on her phone, switching it off. "I do have some ibuprofen and pain relief cream that should help. It may be out of date, though."

Sarah shifted her weight on the couch. "Whatever you have will work. I think the ibuprofen will be enough, but if you have the other, that will be good as well."

Tiffany turned, then glanced down at Hannah who stuck to her like glue. "Move out of the way, sweet pea." Hannah shifted to the side, moving out of her way. "I'll be right back."

Hannah watched her mom vanish into the bleakness of the hallway, and buried her face into the stuffed animal's head as she swayed. Her yellow dress twirled around her waist as she looked over at Sarah.

"Does your friend there have a name?" Sarah asked, pointing at the bear.

Dark Roads

"His name is Teddy," Hannah replied, her voice muffled from the bear's head pressed to her mouth.

Sarah tilted her head. "Nice to meet you, Teddy. That is a fantastic name. I like that."

A half smile cracked over the little girl's face, hidden by the stuffed animal's fur.

"Okay," Tiffany said, emerging from the murk of the hallway. "I've got the ibuprofen and the pain relief cream is still good. There isn't much inside the tube, but enough for a couple of applications I think."

Sarah stuck out her hand. "I'll take whatever you have, thanks."

Tiffany handed her the bottle and tube. "Let me get you some water."

"How is the water pressure?" Sarah asked, setting the bottle and tube on the couch beside her.

"Abysmal." Tiffany skirted the bar top that led into the kitchen. "It's a slow trickle now. I imagine soon, if they don't get the power back on, it'll stop all together. Not that this building has ever had amazing water pressure in the first place, mind you."

Sarah grabbed the bottle of ibuprofen and popped the top. A handful of dark-coated pills rattled about at the bottom of the container. "You don't have much left in the bottle. Looks like there might be five or six pills."

"It's okay. Take what you need. I don't use too much of it anyway, so it'll be put to good use." Tiffany walked from the kitchen with a glass of water in her hand.

"Mommy, I'm hungry. Can I have a snack before bed?" Hannah kept her face buried in the bear, muffling her already soft-spoken voice.

Tiffany handed Sarah the half-filled glass of water, then turned toward Hannah. "A snack? I thought you had one before I left? Besides, didn't you say your tummy hurt?"

"I think it hurt because I'm hungry. We didn't have much to eat tonight. Teddy is hungry too. His stomach keeps making these strange noises." Hannah placed the bear next to her ear and listened.

Sarah popped two of the pills into her mouth, then chased them down with the tepid water.

"I know, baby. I wish we had more food, but things have been tough here lately, and with the power being out, it's been hard for Mommy to find a store that's open." Tiffany placed her fingers under Hannah's chin. "I'll tell you what. I think we might have one of those mini granola bars in the cupboard. Why don't you and Teddy share one. Will that work?"

Hannah turned the bear's face to her ear and acted as though the stuffed animal spoke to her. She nodded, then said, "Teddy likes that idea. Thanks, Mommy. You're the best."

The excited red-headed girl ran off with her arms in the air.

Sarah felt bad for taking up any resources Tiffany had. She knew all too well how hard it could be living on a shoestring budget.

"I can leave. I really don't want to be a burden on you," Sarah said. "You've shown me so much kindness already."

Tiffany dipped her chin, staring at her. She shook her head. "You're fine. Things have been tight for a while, but we'll be okay. We've been through worse and have come out the other side."

"Mommy, we've finished our snack," Hannah said, from the flickering candlelight in the kitchen. "Did you want me to brush my teeth now?"

"You finished it already?" Tiffany asked, shocked. "Did you chew it?"

Dark Roads

Hannah walked out from the kitchen with her head tilted forward–chin pressed against her chest. "I dropped it on the floor by accident."

Tiffany rubbed her face, then asked, "Did you want another one?"

"The box is empty and I didn't see anymore. I'm sorry, Mommy." Hannah looked at her from over the top of the bear's head. "I think I'll just brush Teddy's and my teeth now."

"Okay, sweetie." Tiffany excused herself and followed Hannah down the hallway.

Sarah grabbed the tube of pain relief cream, and unscrewed the cap off the top. She squeezed out a dime size portion into her palm, then leaned forward.

The awkward position she sat in made it cumbersome to apply the cream to the affected area. Her entire body ached from being tossed around by burly henchmen and doing death-defying stunts out of windows into trash bins.

The palm of her hand slathered the cream over her ankle. It covered most of the swelling.

Sarah huffed, then deflated against the couch. The back of her head rested on the firm cushion, and her mouth fell open in exhaustion.

What a day.

In the other room, Sarah could hear Tiffany and Hannah chatting it up. Their voices sounded jovial–a hint of laughter lingered in the gloom of the powerless apartment.

"Be right back, Mommy." Hannah ran down the hallway to the living room with Teddy clutched between her arm and body. Her heavy footsteps echoed through the silent apartment.

Sarah tilted her head forward, then peered at the shy, sweet girl. "Are you heading to bed?"

"Yeah, but Teddy wanted to tell you goodnight before he went to sleep." Hannah grabbed the bear's arm and moved it up and down.

"Well goodnight, Teddy. I hope the both of you get a good night's rest and have some of the best dreams." Sarah couldn't help but smile at the cuteness.

Hannah waved at Sarah, then ran back down the hall at full speed.

Tiffany emerged from the hallway a short time later. She plopped down into the aged-leather recliner, laid back, then turned toward Sarah. "She cannot go to bed without a story or two. She tried for another, but I had to shut her down."

"She's a cute kid," Sarah said. "I imagine there's never a dull moment around here."

"Not at all. She's like the Energizer Bunny at times. Going nonstop most days."

Sarah chuckled. "Yeah. That sounds about right. They help keep you young."

"Or tired." Tiffany rubbed her hands over her face, then dug the heels of her palms into her eyes. She looked spent and tired, but it didn't detract from her natural beauty.

Her skin looked soft and smooth, free of any blemishes. Strands of her light auburn hair framed her face. She looked to be in her early to mid-thirties, or younger.

"Well, it looks like you're doing a good job with her."

"I'm trying." Tiffany rested her forearms on the arms of the leather chair, then glanced toward the hall. "Being a single parent is hard when things are grinding along as normal, but add the blackout and lack of supplies and resources, and all of the crazy stuff people are doing out there, it just complicates matters ten times over. That's why I've left her here alone when I go out to get medicine or other essentials. It kills me to do so, but I feel she'll be safer here than out there."

Sarah nodded. "I can only imagine how hard that must be to do. Some people have lost their minds. I will say that it looks like you're holding up pretty well, all things considered."

"We are." Tiffany looked back to Sarah. "What about you? Do you have any kids? A husband?"

A wave of sadness crashed into Sarah, more so than what had already punished her. She diverted her gaze, staring off into the bleakness of the apartment.

"Did I say something wrong?" Tiffany asked, concerned. "I hope I haven't upset you in any way."

Sarah shook her head, then waved her hand. "No. It's ok. I am married, well, separated. We're working on things, though. It's been rocky between us since our daughter passed over a year ago."

Tiffany cupped her hand over her mouth. "I'm so sorry to hear that. I can't imagine what that must have been like."

"It's been tough, but we've handled it the best we can." Sarah had no desire to dive deeper into such matters. She grazed the surface and offered up what she could in the way of small talk. Going any further into her troubled past or the crap storm that had trailed her for the past few days didn't sit high on her to-do list.

Silence lingered between the two women. The subtle sounds of discord from the outside world fed into the apartment from the cracked window.

Sarah cleared her throat, then changed the subject. "Your phone isn't working by chance, is it?"

"If you mean by having a signal, no. Hasn't been working since the blackout started. My portable power bank is almost dead with no way of recharging it. Soon, I won't even have my phone," Tiffany answered.

Crap.

A big yawn fled Sarah's mouth. She lifted her hand to her face, then remembered she had the pain relief cream smeared over her palm. "You wouldn't happen to have a towel or napkin I could wipe my hand off with, would you? I've got that cream on my hand and don't want to touch my face with it."

"Oh, yes. I'm sorry about that. I didn't think to grab you anything to wipe your hands off on." Tiffany got up from her chair, then walked to the kitchen. "I hope the couch will be good for you to sleep on for the night. I know it's not the most comfortable thing in the world and do apologize for that."

Sarah pressed her clean hand to the stiff cushions. "It will be fine. Thank you."

Tiffany walked back from the kitchen with a rag, then handed it to Sarah. "I just assumed you'd be staying the night, given your ankle and all."

"As long as I'm not intruding on you," Sarah replied, wiping the medicated cream from her palm.

"Not at all." Tiffany pointed to the corner of the couch. "There's a blanket you can use along with some pillows. I've been leaving the window cracked some to allow the air to circulate so it doesn't get too stuffy. If you need an additional blanket, let me know, and I'll see what I can scrounge up."

Sarah looked at the darkened corner, then back to Tiffany. The breeze from outside cooled the apartment, making it comfortable and took the stuffiness out of the air. "It'll be fine. It feels good."

Tiffany smiled. "Oh. One more thing. The bathroom is down the hallway. Also, if you get hungry, there's a bit of food in the pantry. I don't have much, but you're welcome to what I have."

"Thanks. I appreciate it." Sarah had no intentions of taking any of Tiffany's food, despite the grumbling in her stomach.

Dark Roads

"Sleep well." Tiffany turned and left the living room, fading into the blackness of the hallway. Although Sarah didn't know the exact time, she didn't think it to be that late. Maybe around 9:30 or so.

Sarah sat on the couch alone with her thoughts. They sprang from one event to the next going over how they'd shaped her life up until that point.

Despite being tired, she dreaded falling asleep for fear the nightmares would come to haunt her—a never-ending slog through her brain. Now Spencer Lasater, the Creeper, had emerged in her darkest hour.

CHAPTER NINE

RUSSELL

The darkness lifted.

Tiny slivers of sun shone through the gaps between the planks of wood nailed to the wall over the windows. The strident beams of light focused on Russell's face, breaking his slumber.

He stirred–prone on his stomach with his arms doubling as a pillow. His lids cracked open, only to close against the invasion of the intrusive daylight.

Max groaned, then sat up. The German shepherd had slept between Cathy and him—a fixed sentry and alarm system to alert them of any dangers. None came.

The canine's unholy breath blasted Russell in the face. The smell churned his stomach. Still, the smell paled in comparison to that of the upstairs bedroom.

Dark Roads

"All right. I get it. Time to rise and shine." Russell removed his arm from under his head and rubbed under the canine's maw.

Max licked the side of Russell's face, his sticky tongue running over Russell's cheek.

Russell patted the affectionate dog on the head. "Okay, I'm getting up."

Max stretched his front legs, then his hind legs. He gave his coat a good shake, then trotted off toward the foyer.

Every muscle in Russell's body ached from sleeping on the unforgiving floor. He sat up and took a moment to gather himself. He dug the tips of his fingers into his eyes, trying to erase the haze that coated each. His hand rubbed up and down his face as he yawned.

Cathy sat motionless on the blanket with her arms folded across her chest.

Russell didn't want to wake her yet. She needed her rest. He grabbed his piece from the floor and stuffed it into the waistband of his jeans.

Max galloped through the sprawling home, his claws scraping over the wood floor. He tore in from the other entrance to the living room on the far side of the space.

"Exploring, using the bathroom, or both?" Russell asked the excited canine.

The German shepherd spoke, groaning and looking at him with wide eyes and a bushy tail that wagged.

"You're just a bit too excited this morning considering we slept in this dump. I'm going to need for you to bring it down a notch."

Max barked, then spun around in a circle.

"All right. Keep it down and chill out," Russell said. "I'm moving."

Max took the lead and trotted toward the foyer.

Russell moved–each step slow and sluggish. He massaged his sore thighs, then caught up with the rambunctious canine.

The house didn't seem as eerie in the daylight as it had at night.

They headed down the hallway toward the kitchen, then out to the porch.

The cool morning breeze felt good and refreshing on Russell's face. The air smelled clean and free of any pollution that one would find in the bigger cities. Minus the moldy stench of the house, Russell welcomed the fresh air.

He unlocked the screen door, giving the overzealous German shepherd access to the wide-open expanse of the yard, field, and woods surrounding the home.

Max bolted from the porch to the concrete walkway. He cut into the verdure with his nose trained to the ground. He navigated the dew-covered weeds–his tail standing taut as he sniffed about.

"Stay close and don't wander off too far, bud."

Max took off around the corner of the house, vanishing from sight.

Russell stretched his arms, then popped his neck. He focused on the Bronco sitting in the grass-covered driveway.

He trudged down the rickety wooden steps to the concrete walkway. The movement made the soreness in his thighs ache, but it would loosen up soon.

Birds squawked from the large trees near the home. Squirrels darted across the open yard and climbed the trunks.

Russell walked past the hand pump and made for the Bronco. He approached the driver's side, then opened the door.

The power bank rested on the center console. The four lights on the side lit up a bright white, indicating the device had charged to capacity.

Dark Roads

Finally. Something positive is happening, Russell thought.

He unplugged the cable from the 12-volt charger and plugged it into the top of the power bank. Russell dug his phone out of his pants and attached the small, narrow end of the cable into the bottom.

The device flashed.

Russell smiled, then thumbed the power button on the side of his phone.

The manufacture logo appeared on the screen.

Max trotted past the Bronco on the other side. He frolicked in the weeds, enjoying the calm morning.

The phone pinged, following the customary jingle the device played when loading.

Russell waited for the device to load, hoping for a signal, regardless of how strong it was, so he could try calling Sarah.

The blue twirling circle remained–spinning in an endless loop.

Russell dumped the phone and power bank into the driver's seat, allowing it to charge. He ran his hand under the dash and located the release for the hood.

The locking mechanism popped.

The hood split from the Bronco's frame.

Russell moved around the driver's side door toward the front of the vehicle. He slipped his fingers between the narrow opening and pulled the latch. The hood opened, granting him access to the engine compartment.

A look of confusion washed over Russell's face. His arms folded across his chest, fingers rapping against his chin as he skimmed over the mechanical construct.

Russell knew enough about vehicles to be dangerous. The basics like changing fluids, replacing worn tires, and a few other things rounded out his mechanic skills.

At the onset, he couldn't see anything wrong with the wires and steel. It all looked old and aged from the grime and dirt that coated the parts.

Russell unfolded his arms and leaned against the steel body. He craned his neck and looked at the passenger side fender where the bullet struck the Bronco when they fled the convenience store. Everything appeared to be all right from what he could see.

The cables attached to the engine block looked worn, but they sat firm on the terminals. No lose connections or frayed wires caught his attention.

Come on. What's wrong here? Where's the problem at?

Russell took a step back, then dropped to his knees, checking for any leaks. His hands plunged into the morning dew–the dampness covered his palms. He couldn't spot any leaks within the thick weeds, though.

He reached under the grill and touched around the radiator. The bottom felt wet.

Great. A possible leak.

He stood up and glanced over the engine once more. He eyed the radiator cap.

Russell unscrewed the top, then peered into the opening. He couldn't see much of anything inside the dark space, but he figured the vehicle needed coolant.

Max darted from the weeds nearby and lunged at Russell.

Russell flinched and gasped. "Are you trying to give me a heart attack?" Russell asked–chest heaving and heart beating a bit faster. "Again, I need for you to bring down the energy some, okay?"

Max groaned, then sat on his haunches. His hind leg sprung up to tend to an itch on the side of his head.

Dark Roads

Russell rubbed the crown of his head and made his way toward the rear of the Bronco, wanting to see if he missed any bottles of coolant.

Max trotted alongside him, his tongue dangling from his maw. He yawned, revealing his fangs, then sneezed.

"Bless you."

The rear door creaked open.

Russell scanned over the tire jack, lug nut wrench, and some other odds and ends, but didn't spot any coolant.

Okay. Now what?

He hammered the floorboard of the Bronco with his fists.

Max looked up at him and tilted his head to the side, confused by the aggressive action.

"Well, I'm not sure how we're going to get what we need way out here." Russell took a step back, then slammed the rear hatch closed. "Come on. Let's go inside." Russell walked around the rear of the truck and grabbed his phone and power bank from the driver's seat. He closed the door and headed for the porch. Frustration overtook Russell, causing him to mumble under breath.

He tossed open the screen door. Max squeezed past him and darted inside. They moved through the kitchen, then down the hallway. Russell's hand rubbed over his face as he sought to calm his nerves.

Cathy stirred on the cushions. Max stood at her side, sniffing and licking at her face.

She licked her lips, then turned her head away from him. "Okay. Give me a bit of space, boy."

Max laid down at her side with his head trained toward her.

"How are you feeling this morning?" Russell asked.

Cathy stretched her arms, then shifted her backside on the cushions. Her face contorted in discomfort, teeth gnashing together. She reached for her injured leg. "Like I slept on the floor."

Russell eyed her wound. "Is that doing any better? We probably need to change out the dressing you have on it."

"Yeah. I'll get to it in a bit." Cathy tried to lean forward, but grimaced in pain. She laid back down.

Russell shoved his phone and the power bank into his back pants pocket. "Here. Let me do it for you. Just take it easy."

"I can get it. Just give me a second here, all right?" Cathy's voice rose an octave higher, stopping Russell in his tracks.

The sharp spike caught him off guard. He lifted his hands into the air, then took a step back. "Okay."

The aggravation on Cathy's face changed to guilt. She sighed. "I'm sorry. I didn't mean to snap at you like that. I know you're only trying to help me. I'm not a good patient like you."

"No apologies needed." Russell lowered his arms, then stepped toward her. "This isn't the most ideal situation to be dealing with a gunshot wound. I snagged a bottle of Jack Daniels from the convenience store. It may help with the pain."

"Yeah, but it doesn't excuse my curt response. I do apologize," Cathy replied. She shook her head. "No thanks. I'm good."

Russell skimmed over the wound, then walked around her for better access. What few medical supplies they had sat on the floor inside the bag by Cathy's waist.

The gauze packed on the wound turned a slight red. It hadn't soaked the entire dressing, but enough that it needed to be replaced.

"Do we have any water to clean it off with?" Russell glanced at the floor, finding a single water bottle that sat empty.

Cathy pointed at the go bag, then said, "Nothing in there to clean it off with. I used a bit of the water from that bottle when first dressing it. Between the three of us, we finished it off quick."

"What about the liquor?" I asked.

"It'll do more harm than good," Cathy replied, shaking her head.

Russell removed the bandage, then gauze, revealing the affected area of her leg beneath the ripped fabric of her denim jeans. He examined the hole on the outer portion of her thigh.

The damaged skin looked inflamed, puffy and red around the entry point. It didn't look too bad, all things considered, but Russell had little knowledge of this sort of injury.

"Is there an exit wound?" Russell asked, peering up at her.

Cathy nodded. "Yeah. The back of my thigh."

"I thought it just grazed you?"

"I thought it did too, but it caught enough meat I guess."

Russell grabbed the bag and sifted through the contents. He tilted the opening toward the light shining through the window. "Looks like we have a few more pieces of gauze and bandaging. We'll need to get some more. Too bad we don't have any of those pain pills you gave me. They'd come in handy right about now."

Cathy forced herself up on her elbows. "Yeah. Where's a drug store when you need one, or any store for that matter?"

"Speaking of things we need, I think I figured out what's wrong with the Bronco, and it isn't good."

CHAPTER TEN

SARAH

The comfort of the rigid couch waned, leaving Sarah with a knot nestled in the middle part of her back. The dull pain added to the throbbing of her ankle, making for another relentless night.

Light from the window sliced through the tilted blinds, erasing the darkness of the apartment. She kept her eyes closed, fighting for any additional sleep before having to get up.

Sarah laid on her back, leg propped up on the arm of the couch at the other end. Her forearm draped over her face, shielding her from the morning sun.

The city seemed silent–still. No horns blared or other familiar sounds came that one would expect in a metropolis of over four million people.

Dark Roads

Th ceiling creaked from heavy footfalls in the apartment above, then stomped the floor fast and hard. It sounded as if they ran across the apartment, then back again.

I have not missed this, Sarah thought.

Sarah sighed from the annoyance.

Fine. Guess it's time to get up.

A heavy fist hammered the apartment door from the hallway. Sarah flinched. She removed her arm from her face and glanced over to the shuddering door. Her hand reached for the Glock 43 in her waistband, but found nothing except empty air.

What the hell?

A wave of panic slammed into Sarah, but subsided as she remembered that she no longer had the faithful firearm.

Sarah feared that Spencer, Leatherface, or even Kinnerk's men had found her somehow.

"Tiffany, come on." The man sounded perturbed. He hammered the door again, then said, "Open up, now."

Sarah removed her leg from the arm of the couch and sat up. Blood rushed to her foot, making it throb. Her face scrunched in discomfort.

"Hold on and keep it down," Tiffany replied, aggravated. She hurried down the hall, then past the couch while clutching her pink night robe at the center.

"Who the hell is that?" Sarah asked. The haze coating her eyes distorted her vision, making it hard to see. She jammed her fingers into each socket and rubbed, trying to clear it out.

Tiffany worked the deadbolt as fast as she could, then twisted the doorknob.

The door opened wide, revealing a lean, disgruntled man. He stood with his arms stretched out, palms pressed against the jamb surrounding the door. A look of contempt rested on his smug face. His arms flexed as he pushed away from the entrance.

"Will you keep it down. I've got neighbors, you know," she said.

"What the hell took you so long in getting to the door?" he asked. "Do you have some guy back there in your bed or something?"

Tiffany cleared her throat, folded her arms across her chest, then glanced up at the raging tyrant. "No, William. No one is back there except for your daughter and me. What are you doing here this early in the morning anyway beating on my door? I thought we agreed on you stopping by later on."

William stepped closer to Tiffany, towering over her. "Good. Don't forget we're still married."

Tiffany offered no rebuttal.

"Anyways, something came up and–" He caught sight of Sarah and took a step back from Tiffany. "Who is she? You haven't switched to the other team, have you?"

"Don't be an ass," Tiffany said, turning to the side and peering over at Sarah. Her face flushed with embarrassment. "She's a friend of mine. She crashed here last night. That's all."

The deviant looked at Sarah and ran his tongue along his thin lips.

Sarah had seen that look before from the Creeper and other disgusting men who tried their best to hit on her. It never went well for the vile dogs.

"Are you going to introduce me, or do I not warrant such a greeting?" William asked, cutting his gaze back to Tiffany's beat red face.

"Sarah, this is William. William, Sarah." Tiffany rolled her eyes as she clutched her robe. He didn't spot the subtle gesture.

Dark Roads

William waved at Sarah, the smile still fixed on his face. "Nice to meet you. Any friend of Tiffany's is a friend of mine."

Doubtful.

The crude man gave Sarah the creeps–an unsettling feeling that made her skin crawl. The way he spoke and acted toward Tiffany boiled Sarah's blood. "Likewise."

"Oh. I grabbed some bagels from that shop you like," William said, turning his head toward Tiffany while staring at Sarah. "They were giving out bagfuls of the them when I passed by. They're in the hall, on the floor next to the door."

Tiffany rolled her eyes again, then walked toward the open door.

William took off his coat, making himself at home.

The tension in the air amplified tenfold.

"Where's that daughter of mine?" William looked away from Sarah, then down the hall.

Tiffany carried the brown paper bag of food inside, then shut the door. "Can I talk to you for a second in the kitchen?"

"About?" William asked, not giving Tiffany the common courtesy of looking at her.

"Just come here." Tiffany clutched her robe and hauled the bagels to the kitchen.

William glanced at Sarah, then winked.

He drifted back around the bar and disappeared into the kitchen.

The heated words between the two of them grew louder the longer they spoke, filling the apartment.

Sarah tried not to listen, but couldn't help it. She contemplated leaving, but decided to stay, not wanting to leave Tiffany and Hannah alone with William.

95

Hannah appeared from the hallway, her bear clutched between her arm and body. She rubbed her eyes, face still thick with sleep. Her long hair went in all directions.

"Good morning, sweetie," Sarah said, in a soft whisper, motioning with her hands for the sleepy girl to come to her.

Hannah yawned big, confusion lingering on her face as she glanced over at Sarah. "Where's my mommy?"

"Hannah," William called out from the blind spot in the kitchen.

Her eyes popped open with naked fear. She clutched the bear even tighter. Her chest heaved.

"Come here, baby girl. I want to see you," William said, demanding and stern. "I brought those bagels you and your mom like so much."

Hannah turned and fled down the hallway without saying a word.

Tiffany spoke in a low voice to William.

"Don't tell me to calm down. I am, calm?" William's voice grew angrier, more intense, the longer they spoke. "There's no reason for her to be scared. Now go get her, so we can eat this breakfast I got, then we'll discuss you coming back home where you belong. This has gone on long enough."

"That isn't going to–"

A loud crack echoed from the kitchen, like someone being smacked with an open palm.

Sarah stared at the blind corner leading into the kitchen, then asked, "You ok in there?"

"Uh, yeah. Everything is fine." Tiffany's voice sounded unsteady, shaky.

The arguing subsided, leaving muttered voices that made it hard to hear.

Dark Roads

Tiffany walked out from the kitchen and headed for the hallway. Her head tilted toward the floor as she rubbed the side of her face. She trembled and avoided eye contact.

Bastard. Pig.

William strolled out of the kitchen, shaking his head and running his palm over his face.

"So, how do you know my wife?" he asked. "I know most of her friends, and she's never mentioned you before."

Of course, you do. Sarah bit her tongue, fighting back the sarcastic remark that teetered on the edge of her lips. "She helped me out of a sticky situation. I hope I might be able to do the same for her soon."

William grabbed the arm of the rocking chair, wrenched it toward him, then sat down. "And what does that mean?"

"It just means I owe her, is all. She's a kind and caring soul. So is Hannah," Sarah answered. "They deserve the best and shouldn't settle for anything less."

"I agree. I'm a lucky man," William said.

Sarah shrugged. "Sure."

William pursed his lips, tapping his fingers against the arm of the rocking chair. He looked at Sarah with a furrowed brow and a scowl on his face.

Tiffany walked out of the hall with Hannah in front of her. The young girl kept her gaze trained at the floor, face buried in the bear's head.

Both had changed from their night wear into sun dresses. Tiffany's long hair dangled around her face, shielding the evidence that lingered on her cheek from William's heavy hand. She shot Sarah a quick glance through the strands of hair.

William diverted his gaze to Hannah. "There's my baby girl." He leaned forward in the rocking chair, opening his arms to the timid child.

Hannah resisted, sinking into her mother's body.

"It's okay, sweetie. Go see Daddy. I'm right here." Tiffany gave her a peck on the top of her head, then ran her hands up and down the sides of her arms.

"Yeah, baby girl. Come see Daddy." William narrowed his gaze at Tiffany.

Hannah stepped toward his embrace. The look of fear and uncertainty remained.

William grabbed her and pulled her close. He gave her a big hug while whispering into her ear.

Tiffany ran her fingers through the back of Hannah's hair. "Did you want one of the bagels your dad brought?"

"I think she does. She loves those bagels." William answered, not giving Hannah a chance to respond. "Why don't you set the table so we can eat together as a family? It's been a while since we've done that."

"Okay." Tiffany patted the back of Hannah's head, then stepped away.

Sarah stood from the edge of the couch. "Here. Let me give you a hand."

"How's your ankle?" Tiffany asked, looking down at Sarah's feet. "Has the swelling gone down?"

"It's not too bad. I'll pop a few more ibuprofen and rub some of that cream on it in a bit. It's feeling a bit better now that I've been off my feet," Sarah replied.

Tiffany nodded, then headed for the kitchen.

William glanced over Hannah's shoulder as Sarah walked by. The angered look remained.

Dark Roads

Sarah limped around the bar to the dark, cramped kitchen. A mound of dishes sat in both sides of the sink. The counters had a variety of empty boxes spread across its top.

Tiffany leaned with her back against the counter, arms folded across her chest. The dark masked a portion of her face. Her body shuddered as subtle whimpers fled her mouth.

"Did you have some paper plates or towels you wanted to use?" Sarah asked while looking back to the living room.

"Yeah. I've got some paper plates." Tiffany ran her fingers over both eyes, then faced the few cabinets before her.

Sarah limped closer and said, in a whisper, "I don't mean to overstep, but you don't have to put up with that. Nobody should be treated like that pig is treating you."

Tiffany opened the upper cabinet before her without looking at Sarah. "I know. I'm sorry you've had to see all of that. He's supposed to be going to counseling for his anger and all. He had gotten better for a bit, but he's been slipping back into his old ways as of late. Regardless of what he says or how he tries to apologize, I think I'm done. I'm just–"

"How are we coming with getting the table set?" William asked.

Tiffany flinched.

Sarah turned around, spotting the vile man standing on the other side of the bar with Hannah in front of him.

"Just grabbing some paper plates. It's dark in here, and I haven't had a chance to light any candles," Tiffany answered.

"Well, let's hurry it up," William said, motioning for Tiffany to speed things up. "We've got a hungry little girl here that wants to eat. Need to put some meat on these bones."

Sarah grew tired of listening to the dribble pouring from his mouth, and she had only just met him.

"I'm grabbing them now," Tiffany replied, removing a handful of paper plates from the blackness of the cabinet.

"Here. Give me those. I'll take them in there." Sarah held out her hand as Tiffany gave her the plates.

Sarah limped past the bar to the small, round table where William and Hannah sat. He continued whispering in her ear, his voice low and muffled. Sarah set the plates on the table, then dispersed them.

Each time William looked at Sarah, his face contorted into a scowl. Her being there didn't sit well with him and it showed.

"I'll be right back. I'm going to use the restroom, and attend to my ankle," Sarah said, looking back at the kitchen.

Tiffany grabbed the bag of bagels from the bar and placed them in the middle of the table. "Did you want us to wait for you before we start eating?"

"No. We can go ahead. She can eat whenever she gets done primping or taking care of the shiny on her face," William shot back.

"William," Tiffany said, angered by the curt and rude comment.

"Come on. Sit down and let's eat." William dug his hand into the bag, and pulled out what looked to be a chocolate bagel. "Here, sweetie. Got you your favorite one."

Sarah touched Tiffany's elbow, then said, "I'll be right back."

Tiffany nodded, then sat down in the empty seat across from her husband.

William spoke in a jovial tone, acting like them sitting at the table and breaking bread with his family was a typical day's activity. He didn't offer Sarah another glance.

Sarah limped past the rocking chair and retrieved the ibuprofen and pain cream from the coffee table. Her ankle throbbed some, but she dealt with the discomfort. She glanced to the small dining nook and watched the three of them nibble on the bagels as she made for the hallway.

William tore a chunk from the round bagel and gnawed on the cooked dough as Sarah headed down the hall.

Sarah discovered the tiny bathroom and slipped inside. She shut the door behind her, then deflated against the surface. She exhaled the stress and outrage through pursed lips.

A single large candle burned on the edge of the sink, offering a bit of light in the damp, dank space. An array of makeup and other toiletries covered the top. A pile of towels sat near the base of the sink.

Sarah limped past the sink and sat down on the toilet. She popped the top to the ibuprofen and downed the remaining two pills. She placed her foot on the edge of the white-plastic tub and applied another generous coat of the cream to her ankle.

The swelling looked better than the night before. It didn't hurt as much since applying the cream and taking the pills. Plus, taking her weight off of it seemed to help.

The silence of the bathroom mixed with the dimness and flickering candlelight lured Sarah into a lull. She leaned back against the tank of the toilet and gathered herself.

A loud scream sounded from outside of the bathroom, followed by raised voices.

Sarah removed her foot from the edge of the tub. Multiple footfalls charged her way.

"Shut up," William said, sounding more beast than man. "You and me are going to hash this out right now."

Tiffany whimpered and pleaded, but William's voice trounced her words.

A door slammed.

Sarah flinched, then stood from the toilet. She feared what might come next.

Dark Roads

CHAPTER ELEVEN

RUSSELL

Cathy sighed, then rubbed her hand up and down her face. "You're kidding me, right?"

"I'm not one hundred percent sure that's the culprit, but the bottom of the radiator is wet with fluid, so there must be a leak somewhere," Russell answered. "I don't know how bad it is, but we need some coolant. Everything else looked fine from what I could tell, but I'm no mechanic."

Cathy sat up, then slumped over. She yawned, then dug her knuckles into each socket. The skin under her eyes sagged.

"Do we have any water anywhere we could add to the radiator?" she asked through another yawn. "It's not ideal, but could buy us some time until we find a store that has some coolant."

Russell shook his head. "Not that I've seen. The hand pump out back isn't working, and the only water we had we drank or used to clean your leg."

Dark Roads

Max sat on his haunches at her side. He leaned in close and licked the side of her face.

Cathy offered the loving canine a warm smile, then scratched under his chin. "Well, we can assume it's been leaking late yesterday through the night, so driving it right now might not be the best thing. Without enough coolant in the system, it could mess the engine up."

Russell nodded in agreement. "That is what I thought as well."

Cathy shifted her weight, then moved her injured leg. Her lips pursed, and her hand pressed to the top of the entry. "Hand me whatever gauze and bandages we have left."

"There isn't much. We'll need to get more soon, so we can keep that from getting infected." Russell grabbed the gauze and bandages and handed them to Cathy.

Cathy took the supplies and sat them in her lap. "Let me get this dressed, then we'll head out to see if we can find a drug store. There should be one a few miles back the way we came. I can't remember the town, though."

Russell held up his hand, then pointed at her leg. "That wound looks a lot worse than what we thought, or what I thought since you didn't tell me how bad it ended up being. Can you stand and put weight on it?"

"I can do whatever is needed," Cathy shot back, staring at Russell. She dressed her leg the best she could, then tried to stand.

Russell held his hands out, ready to help her if needed.

Cathy grimaced, then sat back down.

"We need to get you some pain pills at the very least," Russell said.

"Damn it." Cathy balled her hands into fists, trying to maintain her composure. She gripped her leg while breathing heavily. "This is total crap and wasting more time than helping. You'll need to head back to that town. Take Max with you."

"Whoa." Russell raised his hands in protest. "And leave you here alone? I'm not so sure that's a good idea with those hillbillies out there."

Cathy shrugged. "I never said it's ideal, but we don't have much of a choice right now. For all intents and purposes, this place is home until we can get that Bronco working. I'm pretty much useless at the moment and can't travel on foot without wasting even more time. It's the only move we have to make. Besides, you'll be able to travel faster on your own without having to help me."

Russell paced about the living room, unhappy with the lack of options before them. He didn't feel comfortable leaving her alone, but couldn't formulate a better plan of action.

"It is what it is, Cage. No use in wasting time on trying to plot out another course that isn't going to work," Cathy said. "This place seems to be secluded enough that I should be fine for a bit. Don't worry. My leg might be hurt, but that doesn't mean I can't defend myself."

"Yeah, still, I don't like the thought of leaving you here like this." Russell placed his hands on his hips, then sighed.

"You don't have to like it." Cathy grabbed the go bag, dumped the remaining supplies to the floor next to her, then tossed it at Russell's feet. "Take that so you can load it up with any supplies you find."

Russell bent over and grabbed the straps. "So medical supplies and pain pills, then food and water if there's space. Anything else?"

Cathy dismissed the question with a wave of her hand. "That should about do it, I think."

"At least take my piece since you want me to take Max. Only way I'm going to leave you here alone." Russell yanked the 9mm from his waistband and presented it to her.

"All right." Cathy took the 9mm and placed it on the floor next to her. "I'd stick to the back road we came in on. Should reduce the chance of you being spotted."

"You're sure about this?" Russell asked one last time. "I had to help Deputy Johnson through the woods when he got shot. It worked out all right."

Cathy nodded. "I'm sure. Besides, you have to come back here because of the Bronco, so like I said, it would be a wasted trip for me. This will give my leg a chance to rest up and heal without putting any undue pressure on it."

Russell slipped the go bag over his shoulders and tightened the straps.

Max sat at Cathy's side, looking at her. He leaned forward and sniffed, then flicked his tongue at her face. A soft groan escaped his maw as she turned his way. His tail wagged in excitement.

"You watch over Mr. Cage here, and make sure he doesn't get into any trouble, okay?" Cathy scraped at the side of his head, then the top. Max licked her face more and stood up. "That's my big boy." She gave him a kiss on the side of his head, then wrapped her arms around his neck.

"Is there anything I can do or get you before we head out?" Russell asked.

"Just get what we need and get your butt back here, so we can leave," Cathy answered, smirking through the discomfort.

"You won't have to worry about that." Russell patted his palm against the side of his thigh. "Come on, big man."

Max's tongue lashed Cathy one last time, then he trotted over to Russell.

"We'll be back as fast as we can," Russell said.

"You better, Cage."

Max trotted off through the foyer with Russell flanking him. They moved down the hallway, then through the kitchen.

Russell opened the back door, allowing Max out onto the porch. He glanced over his shoulder at the front of the house, worried about them splitting up.

Max groaned, then barked from the screen door.

"Yeah, I'm coming." Russell shook the unsettling feeling that weighed on his conscience and walked out onto the porch. "You know your mom is about as hardheaded of a person as I've ever met."

Russell closed the door, then checked to make sure it latched into place. It rattled inside the jamb some, but didn't open.

Max pawed at the screen door while looking at Russell.

"Go on. It isn't locked."

The German shepherd pressed his paw against the screen door. It swung open some. He nudged the door with his head, then darted outside.

Russell followed Max out to the backyard. He stopped off at the Bronco, shutting the hood and closing any open doors. His hands patted the front pockets of his jeans, checking for the keys. He felt the rigid edges of the keys stuffed in one pocket and the bottle of liquor in the other.

Max stood in the grass-covered drive past the corner of the ramshackle home, waiting for him to catch up.

"I'm coming." Russell stuffed his hand into the pocket of his jeans the bottle rested in and pulled it out. A quick sip to dull the stress and take the edge off.

He twisted the cap off, then took a gulp of the brown-tinted spirit. Another followed right after.

There. That should be good.

Dark Roads

Russell wiped away the whiskey from his lips with the back of his hand, then secured the bottle in the front pocket of his jeans.

Max sniffed through the weeds, waiting on Russell to catch up. He sat on his haunches and clawed at his dark-brown coat.

"Waiting on you, man," Russell said, his arms stretched out to his sides.

Max finished tending to the critter biting him, then stood up. He galloped past Russell and took the lead.

They walked the remainder of the drive to the rocky road, then continued on in the direction they came from. Cathy said the last decent-sized town they passed had been a few miles back.

Russell didn't recall seeing any such town that close, but the lack of sleep and rest had his brain fried. Either way, he figured if they moved at a steady pace, they should be able to walk three or so miles an hour.

A lot hinged on them succeeding, and Russell had no plans of failing.

CHAPTER TWELVE

SARAH

The beating of her heart hammered against her chest. Sarah feared for Tiffany's safety and that of her daughter. She limped toward the bathroom door, slow and cautious. The screaming from the other room grew louder, more violent as the seconds ticked by. Sarah listened through the closed door, trying to figure out what went wrong.

William's voice boomed like angry thunder.

Tiffany yelled, pleading for him to calm down, and get out of her apartment.

The demand only fueled his anger and made his voice rise an octave higher. "Don't you tell me what to do. It's you that has broken this family apart."

William had lost control, teetering on the brink of punishing Tiffany and anyone else he laid eyes on.

Dark Roads

Sarah needed to defend herself and her new found friends from the tyrant who had stormed into the apartment.

The knife she took from the man in the alley would have to do since she no longer had her Glock 43 with her.

Crap.

Sarah patted down the pockets of her trousers for the blade, but came up short. It had to be in the living room somewhere.

A loud crashing noise echoed through the apartment. Painful whelps tainted the air.

Sarah took a deep breath, then grabbed the doorknob. She turned it, then pulled the door toward her.

The bickering and fighting from Tiffany's room escalated. The murk of the hallway made it difficult to see.

"Don't touch me again, you bastard," Tiffany screamed, standing her ground against the overbearing and abusive man. "I've had all I can stand of this. No more. Do you hear me?"

The door shuddered as if something slammed into it.

Sarah moved out into the hallway, limping toward the living room. The strife from Tiffany's room continued, then stopped.

A horrible, sickening feeling clawed at Sarah's gut. She skirted past the couch to the coffee table.

"Hannah, sweetie. Where are you?" Sarah asked, whispering in the silence.

The young girl had vanished, making Sarah even more fearful that William had done something to her in his fit of rage.

The dull, nagging pain in her ankle throbbed. She scoured the floor near the couch and under the coffee table, but couldn't locate the blade.

A rush of adrenaline spiked through her veins, making her hands tremble and her mind race.

Come on.

Sarah caught a flash of movement from the corner of her eye. She turned with her hands balled into fists, ready to fight.

Hannah stood before her, clutching her bear tight in one hand and the blade in the other. Tears streamed down her face, vanishing beyond the matted fur of the bear's head.

"Oh, thank God," Sarah said, relieved to see her unharmed. "Come here, sweetie. Let me see that knife."

"Daddy is upset with mommy. He gets angry a lot." Hannah kept hold of the knife, refusing to hand it over.

Sarah kept her movements slow. "Can I see the knife? I'm going to go help your mom out."

Hannah stared at the blade, then back up to Sarah. "Here. You can have it."

"Thank you. Do you have a favorite hiding place you can go to?" Sarah asked, taking the knife from her hand. The fearful girl nodded. "Good. Go hide and don't make a single sound, okay? We'll come find you."

Hannah turned and ran for the kitchen. The darkness swallowed her tiny frame.

Sarah held the blade, then peered in the direction of Tiffany's room.

The discord between the dysfunctional couple remained silent. No pleas for mercy or angered shouting loomed from the hall.

The unnerving feeling that Tiffany met a brutal demise nibbled at the back of Sarah's head. Her fingers gripped the handle of the knife a hair tighter. She swallowed the lump of uncertainty clinging to the back of her throat.

The floor creaked under her weight.

Sarah squinted, trying to pierce the dimness of the narrow hallway for any figures lurking in the shadows. Each step she took, her heart pounded harder, faster.

The door rattled, then swung open.

112

Dark Roads

Sarah froze.

A light flickered from Tiffany's bedroom.

William emerged from the room looking at his forearm and mumbling under his breath. "Damn bitch."

"Where's Tiffany?" Sarah blocked his path, holding the knife toward William. "What did you do to her, you piece of crap?"

He stopped, then flitted his angered gaze at Sarah. "Really? I suggest you lower that blade, and get out of my way before I plant another shiner to go along with the bruises you already have."

Sarah held her ground. Her hand trembled, but she wasn't going to back down. "Here's what's going to happen. You're going to leave this apartment right now because if you don't, I will kill you. Make no mistake about that."

William snickered, then shook his head. "You stupid women are all the same. Not listening and causing problems when there are none. That's ok. I don't mind putting you in your place."

"I suggest you get–"

William stormed up the hall, taking two giant steps toward Sarah.

Sarah slashed with the blade, catching his upper bicep. The serrated edge cut through his sleeve with ease.

He paused, then glanced over the wound in the dark. The vague outline of his face revealed gnashed teeth and a furrowed brow.

Sarah attacked again, trying to find any part of his body with the blade. She thrust the knife at his mid-section, sending him back into the darkness.

William grabbed her arm and wrenched her close. His fingers wrapped around her meager limb and squeezed. "Oh, I'm going to enjoy this."

"I doubt it," Sarah shot back, tugging her arm. She threw a right cross that landed across his square chin. He shook his head from the glancing blow, but recovered quickly.

He punched Sarah in the gut, ripping the air from her lungs. She doubled over, gasping for air.

William knocked the blade from her hand, then grabbed a handful of her top. "Time for your punishment." He slammed Sarah's body into the walls in the hallway, then shoved her back into the living room. The sore ankle gave, sending her to the floor.

Sarah slid across the wood planks–her midsection on fire. She struggled to breathe as the heavy footfalls of her aggressor surged toward her.

"Oh, you're not going anywhere." William bent over and reached for any part of Sarah he could snag.

He grabbed her arm, then flipped her over. His legs stood apart–ten and two. Sarah kicked his low hanging fruit.

"Ahhh." William cupped his genitals and howled. He struggled to catch his breath as he stumbled about.

The knife!

Sarah flipped over onto her stomach and searched the floor for her blade.

Where did it go?

William huffed, then exhaled a deep breath from his mouth. "You're so going to pay for that."

The blade had all but vanished within the apartment. Sarah couldn't locate it in the dull lighting. She crawled away from the irate man, trying to put as much distance between them as she could.

William trudged after her, removing his hands from his aching genitals.

Sarah got to her knees, then grabbed the edge of the bar top. She pulled herself up, favoring her ankle as William grabbed a handful of hair.

He jerked.

Her head snapped back.

She cried out. "Get your damn hands off me, you bastard." An empty glass vase rested on the bar, mere inches from Sarah's reach.

William yanked harder.

The pressure intensified, growing with each violent tug. The discomfort in Sarah's ankle paled to that of her hair being ripped from her skull.

She stretched her arm, reaching for the vase as she drifted backward. The tips of her fingers grabbed the top of the lightweight flower holder.

William palmed her shoulder, then spun her around.

Sarah turned on her heels and slammed the glass vase into the side of his head.

It shattered.

Glass rained down.

His taut hold of her hair loosened, then released all together. William deflated against the wall, then crumbled to his knees. He swayed to and fro before falling back on the wood planks.

Sarah panted, her chest heaving with a surge of energy that pumped through her system. She towered over the sorry excuse for a man, pissed at his deplorable actions.

He writhed on the floor with his hand pressed to the side of his head.

Glass crunched under Sarah's foot. She scanned the floor for her blade.

She spotted the knife a few steps past the rocking chair. She limped over and retrieved the weapon from the floor.

William moaned, prone on his back. Incoherent words slipped from his mouth as he tried to speak through the pain lancing through the side of his skull.

"You should have left when you had the chance." Sarah straddled William's waist, then dropped to her knees. The tiny shards of broken glass bit her flesh through her pants, but she ignored the pain.

She placed the razor-sharp edge of the blade against his throat.

His eyes went wide with fright, lips quivering. He trembled beneath Sarah, a scared little man who now knew the helplessness that his victims felt. "Please. Don't kill me. I'm sorry."

"You are sorry. A sorry piece of waste." Sarah pressed the blade to his throat a bit more. A thin line of blood raced from the small incision she made. "I should finish you off right here. Do your wife, daughter, and the world a favor. One less dirtbag we'd have to put up with."

The floor creaked a warning from behind Sarah. She peered over her shoulder. Hannah stood, watching with shiny eyes.

In that moment, Sarah realized she had become the monster and didn't want to punish the sweet, innocent girl with a violent act that would scar her for life.

"Everything's okay, sweetie." Sarah looked down at the quivering man, then said in a whisper, "You're going to leave this apartment now, and not come back unless Tiffany wants you to. You touch her or that sweet girl again, you will regret it. Do you understand me?"

William nodded in compliance.

"Good." Sarah got off him, and stepped toward Hannah. She concealed the knife, holding it down at her side and away from Hannah's view.

Dark Roads

Hannah leaned against Sarah, squeezing the life from the stuffed animal.

William grumbled, then sat up. He moved in a sluggish manner, dazed from the vase bashing into his skull. His fingers touched the side of his matted hair, probing the bloody gash. He reeled from the touch.

Sarah held Hannah close as the monster pulled himself up off the floor. Her fingers repositioned over the handle of the knife for a better grip, in case he tried to make a play for her. Thin lines of blood ran down the side of his head to his chin.

He looked at Sarah with contempt, but made no hostile advance toward her.

Tiffany emerged from the dark bedroom; a portion of her pink robe hung from the side of her shoulder. The palm of her hand pressed to the jamb, steadying her.

William glanced over his shoulder, a broken and defeated man. A deep sigh fled his clenched jaw as he stormed past Sarah. He jerked the front door open, then disappeared into the hallway.

Hannah broke away from Sarah's side. "Mommy."

Sarah grabbed her arm. "Hold on, sweetie. There's glass all over the floor. It'll hurt your feet if you run over it."

Tiffany walked down the hallway, her hand running along the wall. "There should be a broom and dust pan in the kitchen by the refrigerator."

Sarah slid the knife into her back pocket, then turned toward the bar. She shut the door and limped into the kitchen. The twinge of pain stabbing at her ankle lessened.

The ibuprofen and pain cream must have kicked in, Sarah thought.

Tiffany spoke in a soft tone from the living room as Sarah searched the sides of the fridge.

Sarah's hand plunged into the ether of blackness between the wall and the appliance, feeling for the handle. The tips of her fingers brushed over something round and wooden. That had to be it.

"Did you find it?" Tiffany askcd.

"Yeah. I think so."

The dust pan dropped from the handle and clattered on the floor. Sarah retrieved it and hauled the cleaning supplies around the bar.

Tiffany and Hannah stood on the far side of the apartment, away from the shards of broken glass that covered the floor. She held the whimpering child close to her, then kissed the top of her head. "Mommy is okay, baby."

Sarah set the dust pan on the floor, then swept the bristles of the broom over the busted glass.

Tiffany hugged Hannah, keeping her close to her body. She kissed the top of her head and squeezed her tight.

Hannah buried her face into Tiffany's stomach, wiping the tears that streamed down her flush cheeks.

"Are you going to be okay for a minute while I help Sarah clean up the glass?" Tiffany asked in a soft voice.

Hannah sniffled, then nodded.

Tiffany hugged Hannah, and gave her one more peck on the head. "Stay right here, okay, sweetie?" Tiffany strode across the living room toward Sarah. "Here. Let me get that. You don't need to clean that up."

"I did make the mess." Sarah looked at Tiffany, then asked, "Are you ok?"

Tiffany nodded, then pulled her robe tighter. She tied the belt into a knot. Her fingers massaged the side of her jaw. She spoke in a low tone, so Hannah wouldn't hear. "He's done worse. This is tame by comparison. One of the many reasons that I left him, and why now, I'm filing for divorce. I'm one hundred percent done with him and being treated like that. His second, third, fourth, and fifth chances have all run out, for both Hannah and myself. His actions today solidified a grim future for him ever being able to see Hannah. He'll be lucky to get any visitation rights."

"That would be the best thing. He should be in jail and not roaming the streets. He's a dangerous and deplorable human being." Sarah swept the glass into a pile.

Tiffany placed her hand on Sarah's shoulder. "He didn't hurt you, did he?"

"Not any more than any other low-life I've come across," Sarah replied.

"I feel so embarrassed and horrible that I brought you back here and this happened." Tiffany lowered her head in shame.

Sarah stopped sweeping, looked at Tiffany, then said, "You have no reason to feel bad or embarrassed. He did what he did of his own accord. I'm just thankful no one got seriously hurt."

Tears streamed from Tiffany's eyes. A whimper fled her trembling pink lips. She shuddered, fighting to maintain her composure with Hannah in the room.

She bowed, then said, "Thank you for all you did. I'm not sure what would've happened if you hadn't."

Sarah rubbed the side of Tiffany's arm, trying to calm her down. "I'm just glad he's gone. He shouldn't bother you anymore."

Tiffany wiped the tears and smudged mascara from under her puffy eyes. "Me too."

Sarah bent down to grab the dust pan.

"Here. I'll get it. You just sweep it in." Tiffany grabbed the dust pan and placed the rubber end against the floor.

Sarah swept the pile of shards into the plastic tray.

Tiffany stood, turned, and headed for the kitchen. She hugged Hannah, kissed her on the head, and continued on.

Hannah watched the two women clean up the remainder of the glass, hugging her bear tight.

"All right. I think we got it all," Sarah said, brushing the back of her hand across her sweaty brow.

The air grew stagnant, tepid even. Sweat populated Sarah's upper chest, and raced beneath the neckline of the shirt she wore.

"Here. I'll take that from you." Tiffany took the broom from her hand.

Sarah pinched the front of her shirt and fanned herself.

"Can I color, Mommy?" Hannah asked in her sweet, soft voice.

"Uh, yeah. Give me just one second, and I'll grab your coloring books and crayons from the hall closet," Tiffany replied.

"Thank you." Hannah held the stuffed animal by the arms and lifted it over her head. She spun around, making rocket noises with her mouth, and pretended the teddy bear could fly.

Sarah needed to get moving. Her ankle felt better, and she wanted to get out of Tiffany's hair. "I think I'm going to head out, now."

Tiffany made a wide arch around the bar, her feet pounding the floor. "Oh. You're leaving so soon?"

"Yeah. There's some things I need to take care of," Sarah said.

"How is your ankle? It doesn't look like it's bothering you as much."

"It's still a bit sore, but the pills and cream are managing the pain. I'll be fine." Sarah turned her leg and glanced down at her ankle.

Hannah continued playing with her teddy, speaking to the stuffed animal as if she expected a response.

Dark Roads

Sarah watched with a perplexed gaze. "How is she so calm and collected? I'm still a bit jarred. She's acting as though it never even happened."

Tiffany lowered her head. "It happens from time to time. She's witnessed it so much that she has grown numb to it and bounces back rather quickly. I've tried to speak with her about it and have her open up, but I guess she isn't ready yet. Makes me worried that it's eating her from the inside out. I plan on having her talk to someone when things get back to normal, whenever that may be."

"She seems like a strong girl. I hate that the both of you have gone through this for so long." Sarah spoke in a somber tone. She hoped that they'd be all right going forward.

"You're sure you can't stay a bit longer? To be honest, you're the first person I've had here in months. It's just been me and chipmunk–coloring, reading, and whatever else. I've enjoyed speaking to another adult, though, I wish it had been under better circumstances." Tiffany wiped away the few tears left on her face, then glanced over at Hannah who ran around the apartment with her bear gliding through the air.

"Thanks for the offer, but I really must be going." Despite Tiffany's husband, Sarah's stay had been pleasant. She enjoyed their company and seeing Hannah, and her warm and innocent spirit made her think of Jess. She reveled in the moment.

"Okay." Tiffany leaned forward and gave Sarah a tight hug. "Thank you again for everything."

Sarah hugged her back. "Likewise."

Tiffany removed her arms from around Sarah, then peered over to Hannah. "Hey, munchkin, Sarah needs to leave. You want to come tell her bye?"

Derek Shupert

Hannah twirled around in circles, then rushed headlong to Sarah. She wrapped her arms around her waist, squeezing tight. "Bye, Mrs. Sarah."

The feeling of the child pressed against her body made Sarah's heart flutter with sadness, but also peace. She hugged her back, then bent over to kiss the top of her head. "Good bye, sweetie."

"Don't forget Teddy." Hannah let go, then held her stuffed animal in the air.

"Good bye to you too, Teddy. I enjoyed meeting you," Sarah said, waving at the bear.

Hannah ran off, drifting back into her imagination.

Tiffany walked Sarah to the door with her arms across her chest. She grabbed the doorknob, then turned. The door crept open. Tiffany peered out in the murk of the hallway, searching for her own tormentor.

Sarah touched Tiffany's shoulder. "He's gone, but please make sure to report this to the police when you can. They can help."

"I will. I had plans to do so." Tiffany stepped out of the way of the door. "Take care of yourself and be careful out there."

Sarah walked out into the low light of the hallway. She gave Tiffany a nod. "You do the same."

CHAPTER THIRTEEN

RUSSELL

Russell patted his leg, then dove into the weeds that lined the rock road. "Max, come here." The dense verdure swallowed him, concealing his presence.

Max stopped, turned, then galloped to his side, jumping through the tall blades in a blink. The German shepherd lowered to his stomach, waiting for his handler's next command.

The sound of an engine tingled Russell's ear.

His nerves tightened, and his pulse spiked. He searched for the source, but struggled to locate the vehicle within the trees and bushes that surrounded him.

Russell checked the way they'd come, looking for a trail of dust lifting into the air from the road. He craned his neck and stood just above the tips of the weeds, but spotted nothing of concern.

Max sat up off the ground, resting on his haunches. He skimmed over the area with a vigilant gaze, not offering a single warning of danger being close.

The noise died off as fast as it came, leaving Russell feeling a bit silly and paranoid. Corona and John Deere had him looking over his shoulder for the duo's beat up Chevy truck. He didn't think they'd be around, but it paid to be cautious and alert.

Russell rubbed the top of Max's head, scratching the crown between his ears. "I guess it's better to be safe than sorry, right?"

Max yawned, then groaned. He glanced at Russell with his tongue hanging from the side of his mouth, then licked his cheek.

"Thanks." The weeds brushed against Russell's exposed skin, making him itch. His fingernails clawed at his forearm as he plowed through the greenery to the rocky road.

Max followed him out, then gave his coat a good shake. The fur on his sides had thick stickers stuck in his coat.

"You good?"

Max groaned, then got back on the move.

"I'll take that as a yes."

They followed the road a bit farther before it gave way to pavement. Russell placed the ridge of his hand above his brow and scanned each way.

The road vanished within the rolling hills and dark-green trees that populated the area. Spotting an inbound vehicle would be difficult, leaving only the grumbling of the engine as their warning to duck and hide.

The field across the way had numerous trees and bushes blanketing the area as far as he could see—perfect for staying out of sight.

Russell figured the town shouldn't be much farther, considering they'd been trudging along that back road for the better part of the morning.

Dark Roads

"Come on, boy. Let's keep moving." They walked across the two-lane road at a good clip, then down into the ditch. The pack on Russell's back shifted as he moved up the slight incline to level ground.

Max ran in front of him, taking the lead through the tree line.

The canopy overhead shielded the forest floor from sunlight. A few open spots within the trees allowed thin beams of light to shine upon the ground.

Russell had grown accustomed to the rigors of the wilderness over the past few days. He thought of himself as an outdoorsman, but fate seemed to have other plans for him.

Birds squawked from the thick arms of the branches that protruded from the round trunks of the trees.

A rabbit darted through the low-lying grass ten paces ahead of them.

Max lifted his front paw, head trained at the large, furry bunny that vanished into the tall grass.

"Leave it be, big man." Russell snapped his fingers. "We'll see if we can find some more food for you once we get into town."

The thought of eating a rabbit rooted in Russell's mind. The idea of meat sounded tasty, though, he had never dressed an animal before. Although, he'd prefer a juicy burger with the works and a mound of crispy golden French fries.

His gut rumbled.

Max lowered his head and continued on, sniffing the ground with his tail swaying from side to side.

Russell dug the bottle of liquor from his pants and took another hearty swig. It helped with the stress and dulling the pain in his side and leg.

He gazed at the brown-tinted whiskey sloshing about the half empty bottle.

Sarah pushed her way to the forefront of his thoughts, making Russell miss his wife that much more. He longed to hear voice, breathe her scent, and taste her sweet lips, if only for a moment—a second chance for happiness with the one person in the world that mattered most to him.

The alcohol, though, that swirled in his gut and messed up his life, changed that dream from being a reality.

Russell screwed the cap back on and stowed the bottle back into his pocket.

The dense trees and shrubbery thinned out, giving way to an open field. Beyond the plain, Russell spotted larger buildings that didn't appear to be homes.

"I think we may have found the town."

They trudged through the knee-high swaying green grass of the field, moving closer to their objective. The list of things they needed ran through his head, pushing all other thoughts to the side.

Pain meds.

Medical supplies.

Coolant.

Food.

Water.

Batteries if he could find them, and anything else of use if it presented itself.

The sun lifted high in the cloudless sky and shone down upon them. He hadn't seen the full spectrum of the sun over the last few days because of the dark, plump clouds that had hung overhead, blotting out its warm rays.

Russell skimmed over the area for any movement or threats, keeping a watchful eye out for the two hillbillies or any other unsavory sorts.

Max paused, tested the air, then kept trotting onward. He hadn't offered any warnings, easing Russell's mind some.

Dark Roads

A chain link fence ran the length of the field, separating the nearby brick buildings and the wilderness. Portions of the fence leaned toward them while other sections stood firm and tall. Climbing the wall of woven diamond-shaped steel with Max wasn't going to happen. They'd have to find another way through or go around.

Russell scanned the barrier, searching for any section they could slip through. Too bad the go bag didn't have bolt cutters.

Max sniffed along the base, probing the fence for a way through. He paused, pawed at the dirt just below the jagged ends, then kept moving.

They walked a bit farther before Russell spotted a hole in the ground next to the fence that tunneled to the other side.

Hold on.

It looked rather shallow, like a small animal dug its way through to the bounty on the other side. The portion of the fence's bottom looked warped. Maybe he could work it open a bit a farther.

Max sniffed around the depression, then clawed at the loose dirt. His legs slung chunks of grass and earth under his body and out behind him.

"Hold on for a second." Russell moved Max out of the way with his hand and studied the fence. He grabbed the pointed ends and lifted.

The canine watched with an attentive gaze, waiting for his chance to move.

The fence gave without much effort, offering enough space for them to slip underneath.

Max crawled along the ground on his belly to the other side.

"Stay there," Russell said, removing the pack from his shoulders. He retrieved his phone and power bank from his back pocket, then stuffed them in the side pocket of the rucksack. He shoved the go bag under the fence to the other side.

Russell flipped over onto his back, then pulled the bottom up toward him. He shimmied his way through the gap, trying to void the pointed steel ends of the fence.

The fabric of his shirt snagged and ripped in a few places, but the metal never caught his skin.

Max hovered over Russell, sniffing at his head and panting in his ear. Russell pulled his legs through, then got to his feet. He patted the dirt from his clothes, then checked the torn part of his shirt. He grabbed the go bag, slung it over his shoulders, then turned toward the buildings before them.

The backs of the businesses had dumpsters and trash cans lining their walls. It looked rather clean and organized with no trash bags visible. The outside of the brick structures had no markings or indicators on the wall, making it hard to discern what sort of business operated there. They'd have to move around to the front to get a sense of what each had inside.

Russell made for the pavement that ran along the row of businesses, looking for a gap that led to the street.

Max trotted at his side and didn't venture any farther ahead of him.

His list of essentials shuffled through his mind on repeat, keeping him on task, and his eyes peeled for any businesses that fit the bill.

Russell toyed with the idea of testing the back doors to see if they could gain access, but feared doing so might lead to a hostile and fatal encounter from any occupants inside.

It still remained to be seen if the town had power or not. From the powerless homes and businesses they'd passed since leaving Luray, he doubted the town had been spared from the blackout.

Dark Roads

An opening between the buildings came into view. It looked to be an alley from the doors in the walls and trash cans that sat close to the entrances. They crept to the corner of the reddish-brown brick.

Max stayed glued at Russell's hip, matching him step for step. The duo had grown–reading one another's body language and communicating better, something Russell never thought would happen given the canine's reluctance when they first met.

Russell held out his hand as he toed the edge of the building.

Max stopped, then peered up at Russell, waiting for his next command.

Russell peered down the alley to the street, finding nothing of concern to keep them from going on. A single car faced the road, and a scant few pieces of loose trash skated along the pavement, catching his eye.

He slipped out from the back of the building and moved along the ridged surface of the building.

Max followed on his heels–silent but ready. He panted low, but subtle.

Sweat populated around Russell's hairline and raced down his soiled face. He brushed the sleeve of his shirt across his brow while watching the street.

Russell peered inside the passenger windows as they strode past the white sedan, finding nothing of interest to warrant further investigation.

The road had no traffic, and the parking spaces in front of the businesses sat empty. The interiors of the ones he spotted from the alley were dark.

A bakery, hardware store, and an accounting office caught his attention. He didn't remember coming through this town. Nothing looked familiar.

"All right. Where's the nearest drug store," Russell said, muttering under his breath.

He poked his head around the corner of the building and scanned over the road in either direction. Still, no traffic or signs of people. Strange.

Russell skirted the corner and headed down the sidewalk. At each business, he stopped and peered through the windows. The interiors sat absent of any shadowy figures or hints of flashlights lurking within the dark voids. None fit what he needed.

Christ.

Max stood rigid with his gaze fixed across the street. He growled.

"What is it?" Russell squinted at the pawn shop across the way. The glass door had been busted out. Beams of light traced through the darkness. Shadowy figures walked near the window, then vanished in the murk.

"Come on. We don't want to draw any attention."

Max inched forward.

"No. Come on." Russell rapped his palm against his thigh and continued on down the sidewalk.

Max groaned, then looked away.

They headed down the remainder of the sidewalk to the intersection. Russell scoped out the buildings before moving on. On the far side of the street and around the bend in the road, he spotted a beacon of hope.

Langmoores RX.

The sign rose just above the tops of the structure with an RX symbol etched on it.

Russell bolted across the intersection with Max galloping at his side. Out of the corner of his eye, Russell spotted movement down the street. An SUV headed their way.

They hopped up on the sidewalk and continued moving in the direction of Langmoores.

The grumbling of the vehicle's engine grew louder.

Russell kept jogging despite his ankle being a bit tender still. He glanced over his shoulder, looking for the inbound vehicle.

The SUV tore through the intersection without braking. It hooked around the curb in the direction of the pawn shop. The back end swung outward–tires fighting for traction against the pavement.

Another car materialized in the distance, heading toward the SUV.

Russell focused on getting to the store. He'd only give pause if they zeroed in on him and Max.

They crossed the street and made for the parking lot of the small car dealership just before the bend in the road.

The thick, red, steel beams closed off the drive entering the business. Three rows of various older model cars, trucks, and SUVs faced the street with bold, yellow markings on the windshields notating the special.

At the back of the lot sat a small structure with a ramp leading up to the front door. A plastic closed sign hung inside the glass door of the building.

Max raced up the drive and scooted under the blockade.

Russell hopped over the rusted beam. The go bag shifted on his shoulders, the contents jostling about.

They navigated the maze of vehicles to the back of the property.

A truck drove past the front of the dealership and continued on through the town.

Russell gave a quick look, catching a brief glimpse of the white truck's bed before it disappeared around the building next to the car lot.

Max panted, galloping hard and fast without slowing or breaking his stride.

The duo stuck to the back of the buildings that lined the road and the overgrown field. They plowed through the waist-high weeds without breaking their stride.

No other businesses stood next to Langmoores. The modest white-brick building had no cars parked around the side facing them.

They emerged from the open field, climbed the slight hill of trimmed grass, and ran across the parking lot.

Russell deflated against the building–taking a moment to catch his breath. He leaned forward and pressed the heels of his palms into the soft parts of his knees.

Max panted hard while staring at the road. He glanced up at Russell.

"You good?"

Max sat on his haunches, then tended to an itch on his side. He sat up and gave his coat a good shake.

Russell stood up straight and continued on toward the front of the building. He peered around the corner, and down the stretch of sidewalk that lined the storefront.

A black hatchback was parked at the opposite end of the building. The dark-tinted windows made it difficult to see inside. Russell studied the vehicle for a few seconds, but spotted no movement.

"Keep your eyes and ears open, okay?"

Max groaned.

Russell slipped out from the cover of the building and headed for the entrance of the business. They skirted past the powerless ice machine and cage of locked propane tanks. He looked to the street, then back to the hatchback as they closed in on the entrance.

Dark Roads

The double-glass sliding doors were closed. Russell wedged his fingers between the two sections and pulled in opposite directions. The doors wouldn't budge.

A shadowy figure moved within the rows of shelving and headed to the front of the store. A beam of light washed over the products along the aisle.

Russell rapped his knuckles against the glass, then waved his hand. "Hey."

The figure paused. The light traced across the tile floor to the entrance–shinning in their direction.

"Hello. Yes." Russell rapped his knuckles again against the glass a bit harder. Not in a manic manner, but hard enough to stress the urgency he faced.

The rail-thin man came into view, then stopped. A portion of his face hid among the shadows, revealing only his thick-black mustache and his rounded glasses. He pointed at the sign hanging on the door–well within Russell's peripheral vision.

Russell nodded, then said, "Yes, I can see that you're closed, but this is an emergency."

Black Mustache didn't venture any closer.

"I have money." Russell held up a finger, then dug his hand into his back pants pocket.

The light moved to his hips and stopped.

Russell dug his wallet out, then pressed it to the glass. "Please. I'll pay cash for whatever we take."

The man inched forward–slow and cautious. The beam from his flashlight fixed on Russell's face and wallet. It didn't budge.

Yes. Come on.

He stopped shy of the security sensors near the entrance and said, "What do you need?"

"Pain meds and medical supplies. A friend of mine has been shot. We also need engine coolant if you have any." Russell left out the food and water for now.

The man glanced at the wallet, then asked, "How much do you have?"

Russell opened his wallet, flashing the bills stuffed inside.

"Do you have any weapons on you?" the man asked, glancing at Russell's waist.

"No. I'm unarmed." Russell lifted his shirt and turned around in a circle so the man could see he had no weapons.

"What about that pack?"

"Empty. Saving room for whatever supplies we can get," Russell answered, lowering his shirt.

Max glared at the balding man, growling under his breath.

"Is that dog vicious? If he is, I'm not opening this door." The flashlight trained at Max, blasting his face with the bright beam.

"He's not vicious, just protective. I'll make sure he doesn't cause any problems." Russell rubbed the top of Max's head, then shushed him.

He glanced at Russell, then back to Max. "All right. I'll give you ten minutes to get what you need."

"Thank you. We really appreciate this." Russell peered over his shoulder at the road, looking for the Chevy pickup, or any other threats as they waited to be let inside.

The locking mechanism clicked, then the double sliding doors slid open. The man backed away from the door and stepped off to the side.

Max sniffed at the gap and pawed at the weather stripping.

Russell pulled the door apart far enough for them to get inside.

Max trotted in first, sniffing the checkered tile floor. He glanced at the man, tested the air, then mulled about the entrance.

Dark Roads

"Do you happen to know where the medical supplies are? We'll start there first," Russell asked, shutting the door behind him. "I need gauze, bandages, etc."

The clerk pointed at the door. "Yeah. Let me lock this door first. You can't be too careful. Lots of crazy people out there right now trying to take advantage of the blackout."

"Oh, yes. Of course." Russell moved out of his way, stepping past the security sensors and standing next to Max. "You're right about that."

The lock clicked.

The clerk walked past them and headed around the registers. "Follow me."

Russell fell in line with Max at his side. They followed him through the dim aisles of the store. The flashlight washed over the fully stocked shelves of pain reliever and other medicines.

"Should all be right here." The clerk trained the light at the staircase of shelves, highlighting the gauze, medical tape, and bandages.

"Is it ok if I put what we need in my pack, then we can settle up at the front of the store?" Russell asked, grabbing the straps of his go bag.

"Sure."

"Perfect." Russell removed the bag from his shoulders, dropped to one knee, then unzipped the top of the rucksack.

Max sniffed around the base of the shelves and meandered about the aisle.

The large beam shone over the various products as Russell cherry picked what he thought they'd need.

"Are you from around here?" the clerk asked, hovering over Russell's shoulder.

"No. Just passing through," Russell replied, cramming gauze, bandages, and medical tape inside the bag. "My friend and I experienced some car trouble after a run in with some–"

The light shuddered.

Max growled as Russell felt something blunt press to the back of his skull. A click filled his ears, tightening his nerves.

He froze, then raised his arms into the air. "Whoa. What's going on here?"

"Don't move a single muscle, or I'll blow your damn head off."

Dark Roads

CHAPTER FOURTEEN

RUSSELL

Great.

Russell didn't want to die on his knees in a drug store. His brain worked to find a solution out of the dire situation he found himself in. "Let's take it easy and talk things out, all right?"

"Wallet. Where is it?" the so-called clerk asked, pressing the barrel of his revolver into Russell's head harder.

"It's right here on the ground next to me. Just be cool," Russell replied. "I'm going to reach down and grab it for you, okay?"

Max stood at the ready a few feet away. The subtle growl had grown more intense, vicious. His dark-brown coat melded within the shadows, giving the German shepherd an ominous presence.

Dark Roads

"I hope you trained that dog well because if it comes near me, chunks of your skull and brain matter will be painted everywhere." The man spoke without a hint of hesitation to his voice.

Russell nodded, then peered over to his companion. "I understand. Max, stand down."

The German shepherd's head lowered toward the floor, fangs presented at the threat before him.

"Here." Russell lifted the wallet into the air.

The man ripped it from his hand.

Russell lowered his arm and fought to stay calm. "Listen. Take what money is in the wallet. It's yours. I don't care. Just let us go."

The wallet dropped to the floor at his side.

The barrel of the revolver didn't budge from his skull.

"This is what you had to pay with?" he asked, disgusted. "It wouldn't have gotten you too far."

"Yes. That's all I've got. I don't want any trouble here." Russell grabbed his wallet from the floor.

"Watch it there, pal. I've got a nasty trigger finger." He grabbed Russell by the scruff of his shirt and yanked him off the floor.

Max barked and growled, then moved forward.

"Stop," Russell said, with his palm facing the approaching canine.

The man turned Russell toward Max and used his body as a shield against the agitated dog. His flashlight shone over the canine's face, highlighting the glistening fangs lining his mouth. "Doesn't seem like he listens too well."

"He doesn't care for dirt bags and criminals," Russell quipped. "It's safe to say you fit the bill."

"Funny." The man walked backward with Russell in front of him. "Keep it up, and we'll see how far that sense of humor will get you."

"Where are you taking me?" Russell kept his hands in the air at ten and two.

Black Mustache removed the barrel of his revolver from the back of his head and pressed it into the small of his back. "I'm taking you to the back of the store."

"I'm going out on a limb and assuming you don't work here, so how did you get inside? I doubt they just left the door unlocked, so any thug or petty thief could come strolling in." Russell watched Max stalking them through the aisle. The flashlight stayed glued to his every move.

"Lucky break, I guess." Black Mustache dragged Russell around the end of the aisle where the sunlight beaming in through the front doors couldn't reach.

"Help." A muffled voice rang out in the dead silence of the store.

Russell listened close, unsure if he heard what he thought he did.

"Somebody help me." It sounded like a woman's voice from what Russell could tell.

Black Mustache muttered in Russell's ear. "She must've slipped the gag I had in her mouth."

"Seems like it," Russell shot back. "First time criminal or just inept at it?"

Max advanced, drawing closer to them. The growl remained.

"I will shoot that dog if I have to." Black Mustache removed the revolver from the small of Russell's back, then pointed it at Max. "Don't test me, I'll–"

Dark Roads

Russell dropped his arm, grabbing the man's hand wielding the revolver. He yanked on the weapon, then turned his body away from Max.

The gun fired.

A flash of orange illuminated Max's open mouth and fangs.

The bullet pinged off the floor near the German shepherd.

"You almost shot my dog." Russell gritted his teeth and tried to wrestle the revolver from the man's hold, but the man's finger wedged in the trigger guard.

Black Mustache grunted, then growled in Russell's ear. "My finger." He dropped the flashlight.

Russell kicked the light and sent it twirling in circles across the floor. Blackness swallowed them, then the beam of light erased it all.

Black Mustache punched Russell in the kidneys twice as they stumbled about the aisle.

Russell cringed, a huff ripping from his pursed lips.

Max searched for a way to gain access to Black Mustache, advancing forward, then withdrawing as the two men moved about.

Russell grabbed his forearm, then hip-tossed him into the shelves in front of the pharmacy.

Black Mustache collided with the blunt ends. His finger slipped out of the trigger guard as he fell to the floor.

Max swooped in and grabbed hold of his lower leg.

The man howled in pain as he kicked and thrashed.

Russell gained control of the revolver in his unsteady hands. He pulled the hammer back, bent down, and shoved the barrel into the man's spine. "You're damn lucky I don't kill you right now."

Black Mustache screamed in pain. "Christ, man. Get your dog off me. I had no plans of killing anyone. Ah."

Russell shot Max a quick glance.

He tugged at the man's limb, growling through the mouthful of flesh.

"Where's the woman at?" Russell kept the revolver pressed to the middle of the man's back.

"I'll tell you where she's at, okay? Just get this damn dog off me," Black Mustache answered.

"Tell me where she is now, or I'll have him rip your arm off and use it as a chew toy," Russell shot back.

Black Mustache's free arm flailed about, his hand grabbing at the shelves next to him. "Fine. There's an office at the far side of the store. She's in there. Now get this animal off of me."

Russell pistol whipped him in the back of his skull, knocking him out. "Will do."

Max thrashed his head, then released the man's limp limb.

The beam from the flashlight trained to the side of them, offering a scant bit of light.

"You okay, big man?" Russell looked over the panting canine for any injuries. His fingers scratched at the side of his head.

Max licked around his maw, then rested on his haunches, waiting for his next command.

"Watch him. If he moves, bite him again." Russell got to his feet, then strode over to get the flashlight. He grabbed it from the floor, then backtracked down the aisle where he left his go bag.

His heart raced, causing his hands to tremble from the strife with black mustache.

The flashlight washed over the go bag as Russell stooped down. He scooped it up, slung it over his shoulder, then headed down the aisle.

The woman's voice carried through the store, a bit louder now than before and more frantic. "Hello? I'm in the office in the back. Please help."

Dark Roads

Russell spotted a section of video cables toward the end of the aisle. He thumbed through the black cables fast–finding a fifteen-foot cable that would work for tying up black mustache. Russell lugged the cable back to the pharmacy where Max stood watch over the body. His tail wagged with excitement at seeing his handler emerge from the murk.

A part of Russell felt relieved things had gone as they had. The last thing he wanted and needed on his conscience was another dead body. He had enough of those already to contend with.

Russell secured the revolver in his waistband and set the flashlight on the floor with the beam trained at Black Mustache. He hogtied him as best he could.

The cable felt taut.

Max groaned, then licked at his face.

"I'm good. Just a bit shaken is all." Russell rubbed under Max's chin, then stood.

Oh, wait.

He checked the man's pockets and found his money. "I'll be taking that back." Russell stood, grabbed the flashlight, and headed toward the office.

Max charged ahead, zeroing in on the pleas for help.

"Hold on. Don't go in just yet." Russell trained the light at the wall.

Max looked his way, then straight ahead where the woman pleaded for help.

"Hello. Ma'am?" Russell said, standing at Max's side.

"Oh, thank God," she said, relieved. "Yes. I'm in here. Please help me."

Russell craned his neck, then focused the light through the cracked open gun metal steel door that led into the office.

Max nudged the door open farther with his head. The hinges squeaked in the silence.

Russell pulled the revolver from his waistband, then followed him in. He pushed the door open until it hit the wall.

The woman's feet wiggled from behind the metal desk. Max sniffed at her legs.

"What's that?" Her voice raised an octave, fear gripping her tone.

"It's okay. It's just my dog." Russell patted his leg. "Stop sniffing her." Russell set the revolver on top of the desk.

The woman pulled at her arms and legs, trying to get them free. She rolled to her side to face them.

The light shone on her legs, then worked up her face. A dribble of dried blood trailed from the bottom of her lip to her chin. She flicked her head, removing the loose strands of curly, brown hair from her light complected face.

"Where's that bastard at?" she said, fighting to get her arms free of the rope that bound her wrists together behind her back.

"He's been taken care of," Russell answered.

"You killed him?"

"No. Just subdued him."

Max stood on the other side of her body, sniffing and studying her scent.

"I'm going to untie you." Russell placed the flashlight on the edge of the desk.

His fingers worked on the knotted rope around her ankles. The jeans kept the coarse material from biting her flesh.

The woman wiggled and moved, making it harder to work on the rope.

"There. I think I've got it." Russell untied the knot, then pulled the rope from her ankles. "Let me get your wrists free real quick."

Dark Roads

The skin around her wrists looked red and irritated from the rope grinding against her.

Russell worked the remaining knot loose, freeing her. He backed away, then offered her his hand.

She massaged her wrists, face contorted in discomfort. She took his hand. "Thank you for helping me."

"No thanks needed. I'm glad you're okay. What happened here?" Russell helped her to her feet.

She adjusted her clothes, then stared through the open door. "I'm the manager of the store. Since we lost power a few days back, I've been stopping by a few times a day to make sure no one has broken in. That guy jumped me at the front door and brought me back here. He tied me up and gagged me. Oh, I'm Erin, by the way."

"Russell. This here is Max."

Erin rubbed her wrists, then looked down to her side.

Max inched toward her, then sniffed her hand.

"He doesn't bite, does he?" Erin reached toward his head, but paused, waiting for a response.

Russell grabbed the revolver from the desk. "Only people that deserve it. If he intended to bite, you'd know."

Max sniffed her fingers, then licked the tips.

Erin rubbed his head. "In that case, thank you, Max, for helping me."

Russell tilted his head in the direction of the back part of the store. "I've got that man tied up out here near the pharmacy. I knocked him out, so he shouldn't be a problem until you're able to get the police here."

"Yeah. Not sure when that will be. Can't call them and haven't seen a squad car in some time. Doesn't matter. I'll figure something out. We're kind of on our own here to a certain degree." Erin walked past Max, then around her desk.

Russell moved out of the office, then stepped away from the entrance. The revolver dangled from his hand at his side. Erin noticed the weapon, then stared at him.

"You have nothing to worry about from us," Russell said. "We're the good guys here."

"Isn't that what the bad guys would say to convince their victims?" Erin shot back. Russell stumbled over his words. "I'm kidding. Besides, if you were, I doubt you would've untied me. This isn't my first time being held up or threatened with a gun."

Russell breathed a sigh of relief. "Well, I'm glad you're okay."

Max strode out of the office, sniffed the floor, then glanced up at Russell. He groaned while looking at him with his soulful eyes.

"I know this may seem strange or sound weird with what just went down with Black Mustache and all, but I wanted to see if I could gather some supplies from your store? I have money that I can give you for what I take. Cash of course." Russell waited for her response.

Erin continued to nurse her wrists while looking at him. "That's not something I would normally do, seeing as the powers out and we're not open for business, but you did save my life. So, take what you need, and we'll call it square."

Russell dug his hand into his pocket. "I appreciate that, but I can pay you something."

Erin shook her head, then dismissed the gesture with a wave of her hand. "Don't bother. Like I said, it's the least I can do for you."

"Much appreciated. I'll be quick." Russell bowed, then stowed the revolver in his waistband.

"Just don't clean me out, all right?" Erin quipped.

"I'll try to control myself." Russell took a step forward, then stopped. "You wouldn't happen to know what pain meds you have in the pharmacy, would you? I have a friend that's hurt and we need something to help manage the pain."

Erin turned and walked back into her office. Russell trained the flashlight at her back. The brilliance from the light shone over the desk and walls. She moved around to the far side of the desk and pulled out the top drawer.

"What are you looking for?" Russell asked.

"Ah. Here it is." Erin pulled out another flashlight and turned it on. "I had one with me when I got here, but lost it when that piece of trash jumped me and dragged me into the store."

Russell lowered the light from her face. "That would help."

Erin closed the desk drawer, then walked back out of her office. "I'll go take a look to see what we have. I used to work in the pharmacy at another location, so I'm pretty familiar with what we stock and what could be used."

"Thank you for doing this," Russell said. "You're helping us out more than you realize. I can't express how much I appreciate it."

"You're welcome. Now go gather what you need. I'll catch up to you shortly." Erin walked to the back of the store and vanished into the pharmacy.

Russell patted his thigh with the palm of his hand, then said, "Come on, Max. Let's go shopping."

Derek Shupert

CHAPTER FIFTEEN

SARAH

The stairs in Tiffany's building tested Sarah's ankle. Each step made the injured bone throb.

Light from the bottom floor of the apartment building sliced through the murk like a laser. The heavy footfalls of someone lurking below echoed in the silence.

Sarah hit the landing and froze.

Her nerves tightened, and her heart raced from the fear of who it could be.

Spencer?

Leatherface or his minions?

Kinnerk's men?

The list of thugs seeking her out grew with every minute that ticked by.

Sarah leaned over the railing, trying to lay eyes on the individual skulking about two floors below her. She craned her neck, but couldn't see them.

A part of her felt overly paranoid, irrational even, given that no one had seen where she'd gone after leaving the docks except for Spencer.

The men after her, though, had proven they had resources and the skills to track people down, despite not having much to go on.

The light shone up through the gap between the stairs in her direction. Sarah took a step back. Her mind worked, formulating her next move. She didn't know who lurked below and that made it worse.

The light vanished.

Sarah held a bated breath.

The rapping of footsteps pounded the stairs from the first floor and headed her way.

Sarah raced up the stairs to the third floor as fast as she could go. She paused on the landing, searching for another way out.

The black void to her left seemed endless and daunting.

A light flickered into existence, drawing her eye to the gleam. The rattling of keys echoed off the walls of the hallway.

Sarah headed down the corridor, limping as quick as her ankle would allow. The closer she got to the light, the better she could see.

The shadowy silhouette turned her way, then trained the light in her direction. From what little she could see, it appeared to be a woman.

The beam hit her in the face. Sarah lifted her forearm and shielded her eyes from the harsh light.

A frantic cry fled the woman's lips.

"I'm not going to hurt you," Sarah said, closing the distance between them.

The woman faced her apartment door and fumbled with the doorknob. The flashlight dropped from her hand. She threw the door open and darted back inside, slamming it closed behind her.

Sarah zeroed in on the flashlight and scooped it up off the floor. The light dimmed. She shook the plastic casing, then slapped it against her palm.

The sound of the person charging up the stairs carried through the halls.

Sarah turned toward the landing, afraid of who it could be. The light from their flashlight played along the wall and grew brighter the closer they got.

She backed down the hall, then turned about face. The beam guided her through the corridor and around the bend to the next hallway.

There has to be another way down.

The light shone over the walls, searching for any exit that could be used. She darted past closed doors and a fire extinguisher mounted to the wall.

Sarah moved faster, trying to keep as much distance between her and the person heading her way as possible. She spotted something on the wall ahead of her—a black acrylic stair sign mounted next to a wood grain door that looked different than the apartment ones. Above the door and fixed to the ceiling, Sarah noticed an exit sign.

Thank God.

She tested the handle, then pulled.

The door opened.

Sarah bolted inside the enclosed stairwell. The door closed behind her. Her shoes hammered the steps. Her hand glided over the railing. The light pushed against the dark, guiding her through the ether.

Sarah hit the landing, skirted the steel railing, then raced down the next flight of stairs.

The door from the third floor never opened, easing her mind some.

Sarah hurried down the last flight of stairs. Her ankle gave midway down. She fell forward and reached for the railing.

The flashlight dropped from her hands and clanged off the steps until it reached the bottom. Her fingers tightened over the steel bar, keeping her from tumbling to the landing end over end. Both knees slammed into the dense steps.

Sarah bit her lip, absorbing the pain that surged through her knees and legs. She pulled herself up and bit back the tears.

The beam from the flashlight faded, then died.

Blinding darkness consumed the stairwell.

Sarah eased down the remainder of the stairs, taking one precarious step at a time. The tip of her shoe tested for solid footing before she moved on.

She reached the first-floor landing and felt for the flashlight with her foot. Her leg swept in a wide arch over the floor. It had to be close.

The side of her shoe hit something solid. The object rolled and clattered against the wall.

Sarah bent down, retrieved the flashlight, then backed away to the far wall. She held a bated breath, then looked up through the ether, waiting for the door to open and a light to sweep the stairwell, but no one came.

The door remained latched and closed. A deafening silence filled the hollow space with no footfalls tickling her ears. Her pounding heart swelled inside her head. Perhaps she overreacted and fear pushed her mind and legs to race.

Dark Roads

Christ. Get it together, Sarah thought.

Sarah exhaled, then slapped the flashlight against her hand.

The batteries loaded inside the casing rattled about, but it never turned on.

Damn it.

Sarah moved away from the wall and walked in the direction of where the exit should be. Her hands felt the air, searching for a solid surface.

The tips of her fingers brushed against the wall. She felt for the door and discovered the handle.

Sarah pushed down, then pulled the door toward her. She felt confident that her imagination and paranoia got the best of her, but decided to play it safe.

A scant bit of light caught her eye from the other side. She listened for a reaction to the door creaking open, but heard none.

Sarah poked her head through the opening and skimmed over the hallway. The pounding of her heart lessened, but thumped steadily. Her palms were moist to the touch.

At the far end of the hallway, daylight shone through a window. She squinted and searched for a door, but couldn't see one.

The flashlight flickered, then came back to life.

Sarah trained the light at the hallway and moved out from the stairwell. No shadowy figures or footfalls stalked her in the blackness, confirming her suspicion.

The entrance to the building had to be close. She headed down the corridor, then made the corner to the next hallway. Her lower body ached. Each step hurt, but she fought through it.

A figure moved ahead of her, maybe ten paces or so up the hallway.

She froze, then trained the light in its direction.

"Damn it," the man said, throwing his hands in the air. He turned around, looked at Sarah for a brief moment, then walked back to one of the apartments. He knocked on the door. "Babe, I forgot my keys. Let me in."

The clicking of the deadbolt unlocking echoed in the hallway. He walked inside the apartment.

Sarah continued on past the open door. Candles flickered from inside as the couple stood and chatted in their living room. He gave the young woman a kiss on the lips, then headed for the door.

He walked out into the hallway, then headed in Sarah's direction. The door to the apartment closed.

"Excuse me." The man brushed past Sarah with his phone in his hand. She stepped to the side, allowing him to pass. The flashlight illuminated his way through the hallway.

Sarah followed him to the front of the building. She spotted no other people on the first floor.

He glanced over his shoulder at her, then pushed his way through the single door that led outside.

Sunlight shone bright before the door severed it.

Sarah looked at the staircase, then through the gap to the upper floors, finding no one of interest lurking about.

She lumbered to the entrance and opened the door.

The light blinded her, causing her eyes to slam closed. Her hand shielded her face, blocking the strident rays.

Sarah walked down the steps, then turned past the black steel fence that ran the length of the building. She tilted her head toward the ground and shoved her hands into the front pockets of her pants.

A knot formed in her shoulder, the muscle taut from the stress and constant danger that followed wherever she went.

Dark Roads

Sarah missed Russell, now more than ever. She wanted him by her side to face the struggles ahead, but his status remained a mystery–one that weighed heavily on her.

A horn bellowed from up the street, snapping Sarah from her daze. She flinched. The blue sedan drove past her in the opposite direction, then vanished around the curb.

The mounting stress, lack of proper sleep, and food in her belly had Sarah on edge, moody even.

Hold it together. You can't afford to lose your grip, she thought. *Get home and figure out your next move. Maybe Russell will be waiting there for you?*

Footfalls sounded from the concrete nearby. Sarah caught a glimpse of a person marching toward her.

"Who the hell do you think you are coming into my life and messing everything up?" William asked, standing on the sidewalk before her. "What sort of nonsense did you fill her head with?"

The sudden appearance of Tiffany's abusive soon to be ex-husband made her take a step back. "Pardon me? What are you still doing around here, or did my words of caution fall on deaf ears?"

"You heard me," William answered, foaming at the mouth. "I don't believe I stuttered or slurred my words in any way. You've messed up my life. My family's lives. Because of you, it's all crap, now."

Sarah stood her ground and responded against her own better judgement. "You're the dipshit that's been raising your hand and doing who knows what else to your wife and daughter, so look in a mirror if you want to blame someone. If the phones worked, I'd have called the police and had your sorry ass dragged off to jail. Maybe one of those big, burly men in there could give you some love and attention that you so desperately seek. As a matter of fact, that still may happen."

William chuckled, then shook his head.

Sarah didn't see any humor in the conversation. "What's so funny?"

"You and your big mouth. That's what." His smirk evaporated, leaving only a snarl. "I have half a mind to finish what we started up in that apartment."

"You mean you want me to crush your other ball?" she quipped. "Given my frame of mind, I'd have no problem doing so, but to be honest, you're not worth my time or that of Tiffany and Hannah. Like I told you in the apartment when I had that blade pressed to your throat, you go near them again, and you won't have to worry about being kicked in the balls anymore." Sarah tried to walk past William, but he stepped in front of her, blocking her path.

"We're not done here," he said, clenching his jaw and flashing his gnashed teeth.

"Really? You want to do this on the sidewalk out in the open where people can see who you really are? You're just confirming how stupid you are." Sarah held firm, hoping he'd back off and leave her be.

William balled his fingers into fists, staring at her with contempt and animosity. He showed no signs of backing off. "Somebody should really shut that mouth of yours."

"It won't be you. I can promise you that." Sarah shoved past him.

William grabbed her arm and flung her around.

Sarah pulled the knife from her back pocket and whipped it toward him.

He knocked her arm down, then twisted the blade from her hand. The knife clattered on the sidewalk at her feet. She ripped her arm away and reached for the weapon.

"Oh, no you don't." William bound his fingers into her hair, then pulled up.

Sarah screamed, her hands slapping at his arm. "Let me go, you bastard." She slapped him across the face with an open palm.

William released his hold on her hair, then backhanded her.

She stumbled to the side, reeling from the stinging bite of his heavy hand. The world tilted on its axis, making her balance unsteady.

William kicked the knife toward the fence, then shoved her to the cement.

Sarah caught a flash of movement behind him. A figure dressed in black approached–stalking, preying. The tears coating her eyes blurred her vision. She blinked, trying to clear the sheen away.

"You're going to pay for what–" William took a step forward, paused, then turned to see what had caught her attention.

The man flanking William grabbed him by the scruff of his shirt and shoved him toward the fence.

William hit the steel bars, then crumbled to the ground.

Sarah ran the ridge of her hand across both sockets, clearing the wetness away and getting a better look at the man.

He towered before her, outfitted in the same tactical garb that Leatherface's goons wore. His beady eyes looked into her soul as his hand reached for the pistol holstered on his hip.

Fear took hold. Sarah's mouth dropped open as she scooted away on the sidewalk.

She thought she had given her pursuers the slip. She thought wrong.

CHAPTER SIXTEEN

SARAH

Everyone's brave until they have a gun pointed at their face. Sarah stared at the hitman. She didn't want to be gunned down on the sidewalk like some dog being put out of its misery, but she couldn't control the situation. Her fate now rested in the hands of the hitman standing before her.

"Please, you don't have to do this," Sarah said, pleading for her life. "I'm a nobody."

The hitman held the 9mm in his gloved hand–finger over the trigger as he stepped forward. His blank, emotionless gaze cut right through Sarah, making her gulp. He moved his gun, fixing the barrel at her skull.

William got to his feet, then charged the hitman.

The 9mm barked.

Sarah flinched and shielded her face.

Dark Roads

The single round bounced off the sidewalk, missing her by mere inches.

William punched the hitman in the jaw, then drove him back against the yellow truck parked along the sidewalk. "I don't know who the hell you are, but nobody puts their hands on me."

Sarah seized the open window and got to her feet. She turned about face and ran away. The soreness in her ankle and knees made her limp. She peered over her shoulder at the dueling men throwing punches and tossing one another around.

Another crackle of gunfire rang out behind her. She shuddered, but kept moving, fearful of who had prevailed. She dipped into the alley and ran as fast as her ankle would allow.

Each hard step made her cringe.

A black car entered the passageway at the far end and headed straight for her.

Her frazzled mind worked while on the run, eyes searching the buildings she passed for an exit she could use. No doors caught her attention within the trash cans and black trash bags that lined the buildings.

The car splashed through a puddle, sending a wave of water into the air. Its engine roared within the corridor of buildings.

A fenced off area ahead of Sarah seemed to be her only way to escape the men after her.

The hammering of footsteps stalked Sarah, making her gut twist in knots.

Sarah drifted toward the brick structure, nearing the chain link fence. The solid diamond strand steel had no weak spots she could slip through. She'd have to climb to escape.

The fence looked to be ten feet or more. If Sarah could get a head start climbing it, she could scale it and slip away.

The car bore down on her, running full tilt as she neared the edge of the fence. It came to a skidding halt in the middle of the alley.

Sarah focused on the fence and scaling it as fast as she could. The tips of her fingers grabbed the diamond shaped openings and climbed. The ends of her shoes pushed into the gaps as she pulled herself up.

The front passenger side door flung open.

A tall, burly man emerged from the vehicle. He rushed headlong at the fence with his arm stretched out in front of him.

The fence shuddered as he collided with it.

Sarah held on and continued climbing.

A hand grabbed her ankle, then pulled.

She clung to the safety of the fence. "Let me go," Sarah shouted and kicked at the burly man tugging on her leg.

He pulled harder, ripping her away from the chain link wall. The man's thick arms wrapped around her.

The hitman stood at her side, staring at her with dead eyes. "You're quite elusive, Mrs. Cage. A worthy hunt."

"How did you find me?" Sarah asked, trying to slip free of Burly's large, strong hands. "What do you want with me?"

"We've had men scouring these streets for you since last night. You're worth a lot of money to my employer, and he has spared no expense in tracking you or your friend down," the hitman answered.

Mandy.

"What have you done with my friend?" Sarah shot back, jerking her arm.

"We haven't found her yet, but we will in due time," the hitman replied. He nodded toward the rear of the sedan. "Put her in the trunk of the car."

Burly lugged her past the open door and headed for the trunk of the idling vehicle.

Sarah kicked her legs, thrashing her body every way possible to escape his hold.

The trunk sprung open.

Burly dropped her to the ground.

Sarah tried to run away.

He grabbed her by the forearm in a flash, then pushed the trunk lid open as far as it would go.

"No way am I getting in there," Sarah said, her voice filled with venomous spite.

Burly tried to force her into the black, fabric-lined compartment.

Sarah placed her foot on the bumper and pushed against him.

"Get inside or else," he said, in a deep, threatening tone.

"Go to hell." Sarah tugged on her arm, then leaned back.

"That's it." Burly wrenched her around to face him, then drew his arm back.

"Get her in the car. What the hell is taking so long?" the hitman asked from the passenger side of the sedan.

Burly clenched his jaw, brow furrowed as he brought his arm down.

A muffled report sounded.

Burly flinched. A fine red mist shot from the side of Burly's head.

Sarah froze, panting hard with large eyes.

His hand released from her arm as he crumbled to the pavement.

The hitman skirted the back end of the sedan with his 9mm sweeping the area. He pointed at the trunk, then said, "Get in the–"

Another muffled report sounded. The round struck the hitman's shoulder. He stumbled back into the vehicle, then dropped to the ground.

Sarah backed away from Burly's dead body, unsure of where to go or who fired upon them, then peered down the alley.

Spencer emerged from the corner of a nearby building with his gun trained at the sedan

The driver's side opened. A bald man stepped out with his pistol clutched in his hand.

Spencer fired two more shots, hitting the man center mass before he could squeeze the trigger.

The hitman took cover on the side of the sedan and returned fire.

Sarah flinched from each report, turning and looking for a way out of the shooting gallery.

Spencer fled for cover behind a dumpster while firing.

"You're a dead man, Lasater," the hitman shouted.

Sarah moved around the sedan to the opened driver's side door. The bald man sat on the pavement, slumped over with his back against the inside of the door. Blood ran the length of his body from the two entry wounds. Sarah grabbed a handful of his coat and shoved him away from the car. His lifeless body dumped over onto his side.

Round after round pelted the rear of the sedan, pinging off the car's body.

Sarah stepped over the bald man's legs and slipped inside the idling vehicle. She slammed the door, shifted into drive, then punched the gas.

The sedan took off down the alley with the trunk lid bouncing up and down and the passenger side door wide open. She checked the side view mirror, and spotted Spencer firing from the edge of the dumpster at the remaining men who had tried to steal her away.

The hitman laid prone on his back, still and motionless as she neared the street.

The front end of the car scraped over the slight dip in the street, sending the trunk flapping up and down.

Sarah spun the steering wheel clockwise, making a wide arch into the street. The tires squealed, fighting for traction against the pavement. The passenger side door slammed shut as she straightened out the runaway vehicle.

She flitted her gaze to the side-view mirror, spotting no threats in her wake.

Sarah kept the gas pedal mashed to the floorboard as she tried to slow her breathing. She maneuvered the sedan through the streets of Boston at near reckless speeds. The trunk bounced up and down, blocking her view through the back window.

Her mind raced, trying to make sense of it all. She had somehow gotten tangled up in a dark underworld that grew more treacherous by the second.

CHAPTER SEVENTEEN

RUSSELL

The go bag sagged with supplies. Russell hadn't planned on taking as much as he did, but couldn't pass up the opportunity. A wealth of supplies laid at his fingertips. Everything from medical supplies to batteries to a small assortment of food presented itself to him.

Max chewed a dog treat–devouring the tasty morsel within mere seconds. He licked around his mouth, looked up at his handler, and groaned.

"You like those dog biscuits, huh?" Russell asked, pulling another bone-shaped treat from the opened sack inside his bag. He fed the biscuit to Max, who snagged it from his hand and wolfed it down. "I'll take that as a yes."

Russell shined the light over the contents stuffed inside the rucksack, taking stock of what had been procured. He went over the list of essentials in his head, crossing each off.

Dark Roads

Erin walked up behind them, her footfalls squeaking against the linoleum floor. "You didn't clean me out, did you?"

"I got most everything I needed, plus a few additional supplies." Russell shone the light down at Max. "He sniffed the dog treats pretty hard. I took a bag and some cans of dog food as well if that's all right?"

"Yes. Of course. Can't have that fur baby going hungry." Erin rubbed the top of his head. Max smiled from the attention. She dug her hand into the back pocket of her jeans, removed a bottle, then said, "I found some Vicodin. It should do the trick for managing any pain your friend has."

Russell held out his hand and smiled. "Oh, great. Thank you so much. That will help."

Erin held onto the bottle. "You're shooting me straight on this, right? The only reason I went through with getting you these pills is because of what you did and said about your friend being in pain. If you're looking to just score some drugs for a trip or something more nefarious, then I can't in good conscience give these to you. I'm willing to go out on a limb here since you saved my life."

"I understand, but what I said is true," Russell replied. "My friend is nursing a gunshot wound. It isn't life threatening, but she is in pain. And to be honest, my vice isn't pills."

Erin studied his face for a moment, then placed the orange tinted bottle in his hand. "All right. There's enough in there for a couple of days. Hopefully that'll help her out."

"It should." Russell placed the bottle in his pack, then zipped it up. "I didn't see any sort of automotive section. I'm looking for some engine coolant. You wouldn't happen to have anything like that in here, would you?"

"We don't really carry anything like that. Our supply of car related products is limited at best." Erin pointed to the west side of the building. "There's a gas station up the road some that has a garage attached to it. They–"

She paused. A puzzled look washed over her face.

"What's wrong?" Russell asked.

Erin glanced to the front of the store at the double sliding glass doors. "Thought I heard something. A knocking sound of some sort. Guess I'm just hearing things."

Russell peered down the aisle to the entrance of the store, scanning for any people mulling about or vehicles driving through the parking lot. He didn't spot anything, but did hear a faint tapping sound.

"It's probably nothing. This building is notorious for making strange noises. During the day, when we're open for business, it's not as noticeable, but when we're closed and it's quiet, you can hear it. Might be the ghost the employees say lives here," Erin said, smirking.

"Coming into town, I spotted people inside a pawn shop. They looked like they were robbing the joint. Then this black SUV came barreling down one of the side streets and pulled up next to the entrance." Russell's mind worked, thinking the oddity might be more than just a random noise that plagued the building.

Erin's mouth dropped open. "Are you kidding me? I haven't ventured anywhere else in town except for this store since the power went out. I've been worried that might happen. We have some sketchy folks that live around these parts. They always look like they're up to no good."

Russell turned, then trained the flashlight at the back of the store. The knocking sound stopped, then picked up again. "Did you want me to hang around for a minute and walk out with you?"

"If you don't mind." Erin folded her arms across her chest and pulled them tight. "I need to figure out what to do with you know who in the back. I had to gag him. He wouldn't shut up, and I got tired of listening to him threaten me."

"How far is the police station from here?" Russell asked. "Maybe we can–"

"Oh, great." Erin nodded at the entrance. "Is that the same black SUV you spotted earlier?"

Russell turned and spotted a black SUV pulling into the parking lot. "It looks to be."

Erin trembled, watching the vehicle head toward the store. "What are we going to do? Maybe they're just driving around and will leave. After all, my car's parked out front, so they'll see someone is here."

Max stood rigid at Russell's side, staring at the inbound SUV.

Russell slung the rucksack over his shoulders, then retrieved the revolver from his waistband. He popped the cylinder out to the side, taking stock of the bullets loaded within. "I doubt that'll deter them from trying to do anything to your store. I'm inclined to think the worst and hope for the best. Besides, with the police not being anywhere around at the moment, it'd be the perfect time for them to hit these businesses. Alarms won't be working, and calling the police isn't an option, not unless you have a HAM radio or something similar. Our best bet is to head to the back of the store and sneak out."

Erin didn't seem keen on leaving the store from the look on her face, but she nodded in agreement. "Corporate is going to lose it if they do any damage to the store. That's the main reason I've come up here to check on things. I know how they'd react to suffering any losses, regardless of the reason."

"Cover the front of your flashlight." Russell pressed his palm over the beam, reducing the light's footprint. Erin followed suit. "How do we get to the back entrance of the store?"

"There's a door near my office that leads to the stock room. It's pretty messy back there at the moment. We received a shipment of product the day we lost power, so there are pallets and boxes all over the receiving area," Erin answered.

The SUV pulled close to the building, stopping shy of the bright-yellow concrete pillars in front of the double sliding doors. The headlights flicked on, casting its high intensity beams inside the store's dark interior.

Russell ducked.

Erin mimicked him.

Max growled a bit louder.

They stooped in the aisle, then retreated toward the back of the store. The light from the vehicle drew close to their position, but faded before reaching them.

Erin skirted the edge of the shelving and hid behind the endcap.

Max and Russell took cover behind the shelving at the end of the aisle next to them.

"What are they doing?" Erin stayed out of sight with her hand still pressed to the end of the flashlight.

Russell moved Max out of the way, then peered around the edge of the shelving.

A shadowy figure stood at the glass doors, looking inside. The headlights shining behind him made it difficult to make him out.

He hammered the door.

Max teetered on the edge of barking, his growls growing more intense.

"Shhhh." Russell pet the top of his head to keep him calm and collected.

Dark Roads

The man pounded the glass door again, then waited for a response.

"I guess they're trying to see if anybody is here or not," Russell said.

Black Mustache's muffled voice tingled his ear.

Russell looked toward the pharmacy, spotting the shadowy silhouette of his body. "Where's the bathroom at?"

"In the corner, just past the pharmacy there," Erin replied.

"All right. Wait here. Max, stay quiet."

"What are you doing?" Erin asked, puzzled.

"I'm going to move Black Mustache inside the bathroom, so they don't spot him right away. I doubt that'll be one of their main places to check." Russell thumbed the switch to his flashlight, then crammed the revolver in his waistband. He skulked through the blackness to the bound and gagged man.

His vision had grown accustomed to the lack of light. The vague shapes of the shelves and other items offered a subtle layout of the store.

Russell grabbed what little bit of cable he could near Black Mustache's feet, and dragged him across the floor toward the bathroom.

The hammering from up front ceased.

Russell turned his head to the side, but couldn't lay eyes on the entrance.

What are they up to?

Black Mustache jerked his arms, and tried to speak through the rag Erin stuffed his mouth with.

"Pipe down, will ya?" Russell turned the light back on, keeping the beam trained at the floor. He backed into the bathroom door, pushing it open.

Black Mustache thrashed, fighting to free his arms and legs. The cable bound around his ankles and wrists held firm.

The scent of cleaning agents and a hint of lavender permeated the air. Russell's boots squeaked against the floor.

Russell placed Black Mustache under the sink, then patted him on the top of his head. "Take a nap or something. We'll send the cops by to pick you up a bit later."

Black Mustache turned his head to the side, then tried to look up at Russell. He screamed through the gag, tugging at his wrists.

Russell left him to the confines of the small restroom and headed out. He pulled the door open, then raced back over to Max's side. "We should be good for a bit."

"Come on. I'll take us to the receiving area." Erin backed away from the shelving.

"Go on." Russell patted Max's side, sending him darting across the aisle to Erin.

He peered at the front entrance, watching two men fiddle with the door. They had something jammed in the crevasse–perhaps a crowbar or something of the sort to pry it open.

Russell palmed his light and ran past the aisle, catching up with Erin and Max.

They sprinted along the back wall, past her office, to the lone black door.

Erin pushed her way through the dense, plastic, swinging door.

Max stayed on her heels.

A loud banging noise sounded from the front of the store, stopping Russell shy of the stock room. He craned his neck, trying to peer over the shelves, but couldn't clear the tops of the mountainous racks.

"Watch your step back here. It's a cluttered mess," Erin said.

Dark Roads

Russell slipped inside the receiving area, allowing the door to swing about on its hinges.

The lack of air circulating made it warm inside the enclosed building. The stock room felt worse, stifling even.

Erin navigated the maze of pallets and stacks of boxes covering the floor. She skirted past mounds of flattened boxes that had been emptied out.

A row of steel beams and racks ran the length of the wall that butted up to the pharmacy. Each section sat fully stocked with an array of products.

A scant bit of light shone through the edges around the roll up bay door they passed, bleeding into the stock room.

"The receiving door is right up here." Erin trained the light ahead of them, cutting through the shadows.

Max paused, stopping dead in his tracks.

"What is it?" Russell asked, taking a knee at his side. "Hold up a minute."

Erin turned around. She shined her light at them. "What's wrong?"

"He's picked something up."

Derek Shupert

CHAPTER EIGHTEEN

RUSSELL

Max lowered his head and focused his gaze in the direction of the receiving door. His body tensed, muscles taut. He took a step forward, then growled.

The receiving door shuddered.

Erin turned toward the noise, then gasped. Her light trained on the gunmetal surface and held.

"They're out back as well," she said, in a frightened whisper. The door pushed out, but the deadbolt kept it from opening.

"Aside from the front entrance and the receiving door, is there another exit we could use?" Russell asked.

Erin shook her head. "Just those two and well, the roll up door. We have an emergency exit, but the door is messed up and won't open. It hasn't been fixed yet."

Great.

The people outside the rear of the store continued messing with the door. The sound of metal scraping over the exterior surface made Russell cringe–like fingernails over a chalkboard.

"Okay. We need to find a place to hold up," Russell said. "Can your office door be locked?"

Erin nodded. "It's got a deadbolt on it."

"Good. Come on." Russell grabbed Max by his collar and turned him around. The agitated German shepherd obeyed without resistance and followed his lead.

Russell moved through the maze of pallets to the swinging door. He pushed it open to the sound of shattering glass. "Hurry up."

They hurried along the back wall to Erin's office. The crunching of glass filled Russell's ears. He thumbed his flashlight off and stowed it in the back pocket of his jeans.

He stood to the side of the door, motioning for Erin to get inside.

She killed her light and entered the ether of blackness.

"Lock this door and stay quiet," he whispered. "There are no windows, so they won't be able to see inside. Jam a chair under the handle if you need to, just be as quiet as possible."

"Are you not coming inside?" Erin stood in the blinding darkness, the vague outline of her frame visible.

"I'm going to try and draw them away from here, but I want you safe." Russell grabbed the handle and pulled the door toward him.

Erin caught the door with the side of her foot. "Just come in here where it's safe."

"Don't worry. Everything is going to be fine. I promise," Russell replied, reassuring her the best he could.

Erin removed her foot, and Russell closed the door.

The deadbolt clicked. He tested the handle to be sure. The door didn't budge.

Dark Roads

"Come on, Max." Russell patted his leg, then ran away from the office. His mind worked to plot out some sort of game plan to rid the store of the vandals.

Lights moved around in the air, cutting through the darkness with ease. The beams helped to track their movement and positions within the building.

Max stayed at his handler's side, mimicking his every move as they skulked through the blackness.

Russell darted past the entrance to the receiving area, catching multiple beams of light from under and around the swinging door. By his count, at least four men had breached the building.

The intruders' voices carried throughout the store, barking at one another in a hostile manner.

"I don't give two shits about packs of smokes or anything of the sort," a raspy voice said, shouting loud. "We're not here for that– only the money. Plain and simple. That car out front belongs to the manager of the store. Bill should've stopped by earlier to check things out. I'm not sure where the hell he's at, but we need to search the store to see if we can find her. Just because the cops aren't around at the moment doesn't mean they won't drop in on us, so we need to move fast."

Russell crept along the aisle on the far side of the store– away from the main entrance and stock room. His fingers adjusted over the grip of the revolver. He drew a sharp breath and held it for a moment.

Think, think, think, Russell said, to himself.

He had no intentions of gunning down the men if he didn't have to, but would if it meant the difference between Erin, Max, and Russell living or dying.

Derek Shupert

A light traced along the floor that ran in front of the aisle Russell and Max took cover behind. The strident beam grew brighter. Footfalls squeaked against the tile, drawing closer to them.

Max growled, low and subtle.

Russell shushed him as they neared the edge of the shelving– the revolver trained dead ahead. He paused, stooped down some, then peered through the gap between the shelves. His body stayed hidden–concealed by the steel rack and various dry goods stacked in nice, neat rows. The revolver had just four rounds left. He'd have to make each shot count.

The man stopped shy of the aisle on the other side. His light swept the dark corner in front of him, illuminating the small photo center area. The beam focused on the counter, then the cash register that sat hidden among the pamphlets and other marketing materials. He walked toward the counter and scanned over the register.

Russell stepped out from the aisle, then looked to the sunlight that shone through the busted doors. He didn't spot any movement near the opening. No black clad figures moved in the murk. He had his window to strike while the man had his back turned to him.

His pulse spiked with each step he took toward the distracted man. He shifted his gaze to the entrance of the store, then back to his target.

The light sat on the counter, facing the register and wall lined with an array of camera accessories and printing products. The man leaned over the top of the counter, messing with something hidden from Russell's sight. His rail-thin frame shifted from side to side as he jerked his arms.

Russell stalked the man with the revolver trained at the back of his skull.

"Screw this." The man stood up straight, grabbed the light, then took a step back from the edge of the counter.

Dark Roads

Russell struck the back of his head with the base of the revolver's grip–hard and violent.

A faint yelp fled the man's lips. His knees buckled. The flashlight dropped from his hand and hit the floor.

Damn it.

Russell caught him by the arms before he hit the ground. He dragged the unconscious man's body back down the aisle, then laid him on the floor.

Max sniffed his body, then pawed at his long-sleeve shirt.

The shadow of a figure loomed on the wall at the entrance of the building. It paused, then moved inside the store.

Russell stepped around Max, then made for the flashlight that sat on the floor. He retrieved the light, then thumbed the switch.

The beam vanished, allowing the darkness to cast its shroud over him.

The figure casting the shadow crunched through the shards of broken glass. He stopped inside the entryway and skimmed over the store.

Russell stayed low and retreated to the far aisle. He patted the man down, feeling for a weapon, but came up empty.

A loud banging noise sounded from the back of the building.

Erin.

Russell moved down the length of the aisle toward the back of the store with Max fixed on his heels. They neared the end of the aisle and held their positions.

One of the vandals stood in front of Erin's office, hammering the door with his fists. The flashlight rested on its side, trained at the scarred and scuffed surface of the door.

A portion of the light lit up the black ski mask he wore and the crowbar clutched in his hand. He lifted it over his head, then swatted at the handle. The steel end clanged off the silver handle and the exterior of the door.

Light shone from the pharmacy out to the store. A shadowy figure walked out from behind the counter and stopped. "Hey, stop that for a second, will ya?"

Ski-mask struck the handle one last time, then turned toward him. "Why? There could be something of value in here. Why else would it be locked?"

"Just hold on. I thought I heard something back here." He stood still, just beyond the entrance to the pharmacy. The light shifted in the direction of the bathroom, illuminating the sign on the door. "I think someone's in there."

"Then go check it out and see," Ski-mask replied.

The figure moved toward the bathroom, opened the door, then disappeared inside.

Russell skirted the end of the shelving and ran toward Erin's office with the revolver trained dead ahead.

Max galloped past Russell, his claws scraping off the floor.

Ski-mask froze with the crowbar above his head, then turned toward them. "What the—" He swung at the air, missing the top of Max's head and hitting the shelves in front of Erin's office.

Max bit his lower leg and thrashed his head.

The door to the bathroom creaked open.

Russell fired to the side of the door, sending the men retreating back into the restroom. The report echoed through the building.

"What the hell is going on back there?" a loud, angry voice asked. "Who's firing?"

"Ah. Get this damn dog off me." Ski-mask tugged at his leg.

Max dragged him away from the door with ease.

Ski-mask took another swing at the German shepherd.

Russell blocked his arm, ripped the crowbar from his hands, then punched him in the face.

Ski-mask lost his balance and fell to the floor.

Max released his leg and lunged at the man's flailing arms.

"It's me. Open up." Russell hammered the door with his fists.

The deadbolt clicked.

Erin cracked the door, then peered around the edge. "Who's firing?"

Russell pushed the door open farther, then reached inside. "Come on. I think we can slip out of the back, but we need to go now."

"Will someone tell me what the hell is happening back there?" The angered voice drew closer, the light playing off the floor from down the aisle to their left.

The bathroom door opened again. Flashes of muzzle fire lit up the interior, followed by the crackle of the weapon discharging.

The bullet went wide, missing them by a good foot or more.

Russell found Erin's wrist and pulled her out of her office. He returned fire. "Max, come."

Ski-mask wailed in agony from the flat of his back, trying to rid himself of the protective canine.

Max released his forearm, barking and growling at the injured man. He inched toward the light, the beam growing larger and brighter.

"Max, now," Russell said, stern and direct.

Erin ran hard for the receiving door as Russell covered their retreat.

The revolver moved from the bathroom to the aisle where the light traced their way, then back again. The cylinder sat ready with just two rounds remaining. Russell's finger hugged the trigger, ready to squeeze if need be.

Max turned and galloped to his handlers' side, obeying his command for obedience. He followed Erin into the low light of the stock room and vanished.

"I don't know who you are, but you're a dead man, pal." The tone of the mysterious figure concealed by the shelves raised an octave–filled with rage and hate. The light from his flashlight pointed at the floor beyond the end of the aisle, then trailed toward Russell as he peered around the edge of the shelves.

Russell struggled to get a clean look at the man's face from the shadows shrouding him. The beam from his light blinded Russell as he backed through the swinging door.

The receiving door sat open, allowing the sun's rays to shine inside the small, cramped area.

Max barked from across the way, racing back and forth with Erin waving him down. They slipped through the open door and out of his sight.

Russell navigated through the boxes. The additional light made it easier to see the full scope of the cluttered mess that carpeted the area.

The dense plastic door slammed against the wall. Russell flinched, then looked over his shoulder. A large swath of light shone through the opening, followed by a shadowy figure rushing headlong from the main sales floor.

The man in pursuit of Russell fired his pistol.

The round punched the pallet of products that waited to be unwrapped and worked.

Russell lowered his head and focused on the exit. He ran out into the sunlight, leaving the drug store behind him.

"Thank God you're okay," Erin said, breathless.

Max stood at her side, pacing about.

"I'll draw them away. Head around the building there and go straight to the police station." Russell fired a single round at the opening of the stock room, halting the vandal's pursuit and buying them a bit more time. "Go now."

Erin offered a grateful smile, then backed away toward the far corner of the building. "Thank you."

Russell nodded. "You're welcome, now go."

CHAPTER NINETEEN

RUSSELL

Erin skirted the corner of the drug store, leaving Russell and Max to deal with the unscrupulous thugs.

Max faced the receiving door, barking and growling from the movement inside the building.

An arm stretched around the blind corner of the jamb; a pistol clutched in his black-gloved hand.

The gun fired.

The round missed them by a mile.

Russell had one round left chambered in the wheel of his revolver. He held return fire–unable to get a clear shot. He back peddled away from the drugstore and ran in the opposite direction.

Max galloped at his side.

The men rushed out of the stock room and into broad daylight. Russell counted two, leaving the others inside the business. They swept the area with weapons up and at the ready.

Dark Roads

"Over there," one of the men shouted.

Russell skirted the side of the dumpster that sat at the far corner of the small drive behind the building. He kept his head low and ran at full tilt.

Max galloped at full stride with his tongue dangling from the side of his mouth.

A crackle battered the air in their wake, followed by a sharp ping that made Russell flinch. The round bounced off the steel waste container.

The go bag jostled about on Russell's shoulders. Every step made the pack seem heavier, more cumbersome to lug while running. He contemplated ditching the bag and coming back for it, but didn't want to take the chance of not getting back to it.

The uneven ground of the open field they ran through tested Russell's stamina and the soreness in his side and legs. He ignored it and pushed onward.

Russell contemplated forgoing the engine coolant and just heading back to Cathy, but curbed that notion fast. They had more to lose by being stranded at that abandoned house.

The men trailing them fired. Each report made Russell flinch. Bullets zipped past him, grazing past his arm and waist.

Max maintained his stride, matching each step of Russell's.

A row of buildings followed the curve of the street that ran in front of each business. It would provide cover. The uneven ground turned to solid pavement. Russell's boots hammered the unforgiving tar beneath him.

They ran hard and fast, trying to lose their pursuer. He glanced over his shoulders to gauge the distance between them.

The gap widened as the men in tow slowed some. Their mouths gaped open. For now, Russell had the upper hand and just had to push harder than those trailing them.

Russell lost sight of them behind the corner of the alley they entered. His heavy footfalls echoed with each step. He searched the buildings on either side for an entrance or any hiding place they could use to lay low.

A door cracked open about fifteen paces ahead of them.

Russell stopped, then brought his revolver to bear, hoping he wouldn't have to use his last round.

An older gentleman walked out from the edge of the steel door, then peered down the alley. The thick, black rimmed glasses sat low on the bridge of his nose. What little bit of hair he had combed over the top of his balding head blew in the little bit of wind.

His eyes widened, naked fear lingering in the depths of each sunken socket. He reeled, stumbling back into the building. The tips of his skeletal fingers clutched the side of the door.

"No, wait, please," Russell said, pleading and lowering his revolver.

The old man continued shutting the door.

Russell ran harder and reached for the rickety silver handle.

Max wedged his body in the opening, stopping the door from closing all the way.

"Please don't kill me." The old man released the door and backed away.

"Max, go," Russell said, nudging the canine in his back side with his knee.

Max trotted inside, past the trembling old man.

Russell shut the door behind him, turned about face, and deflated against the interior of the door. He placed his finger to his lips, shushing the quaking man.

"Take what you want, but please don't hurt me. I don't have anything of value. No cash or anything else worth wasting your time with," he said, loud and frantic.

Dark Roads

"I'm not going to hurt you," Russell replied, breathless. His chest heaved, lungs aching. He took a deep breath. "I just need for you to be quiet and cut the chatter for a few, all right?"

The room they stood in smelled of moth balls and mold mixed with a side of chopped onions. The stench placed a strangle hold on Russell's nose and churned his stomach.

Sunlight shone through the windows lining the front of the building, offering a hint at the layout of the small office space.

The hammering of footfalls grew louder from just outside the building, tightening Russell's stranglehold on the grip of the revolver.

Max panted hard, then reeled his dangling tongue back inside his mouth. A subtle growl loomed from his throat.

"Everyone be cool and remain quiet," Russell whispered.

"Why? Does this have anything to do with the gunshots I heard a few moments ago?" The old man spoke loudly, as if he hadn't heard a word that had been said.

Russell shushed him again. "If you don't keep your voice down, they're going to hear you, and then we're all screwed."

"I don't know what sort of trouble you and your four-legged friend here got into, but I want no part of it. Please leave."

"Just because I'm not a low-life degenerate like those thugs outside, doesn't mean I'm not willing to do what is needed to keep me and mine safe," Russell shot back. "I have no desire to hurt you, and we will leave once the coast is clear, but if you don't lower your damn voice and settle down, I'm going to have to shut you up. Are we clear?"

The old man nodded, then took a hefty step back. His frail frame melded into the dimness of the office.

Russell nodded at the main entrance. "Is that door secured?"

"Yes. It should be." He adjusted the thick-rimmed glasses, then folded his meager arms across his chest. "I was on my way out when I heard the gunshots, then I spotted you two running down the alley."

The black SUV drove past the windows. Its brake lights flashed before disappearing beyond the building. The blinds tilted downward, restricting anyone from being able to see inside the building.

"How far is the nearest gas station from here?" Russell asked, stepping away from the door. "I'm looking for one with a mechanic shop attached to it."

"Billet's is right up the street on the left side of the road. Can't miss it, but they're not open with the power being out, much like everything else."

Russell nodded and kept a watchful eye on the entrance. He locked the side door, then walked past the disgruntled man who huffed as he strolled by.

Max followed close behind, sniffing the ground and investigating the desks and chairs that sat empty.

"Make sure your dog doesn't piss on my carpet. I don't have anything to clean up that mess, and don't want my office smelling like a urinal." The old man sighed and pointed at Max.

"I'll try to make sure he doesn't take a steaming crap or piss on your carpet," Russell quipped without looking back.

Crotchety old man. It can't smell any worse than it already does.

The side door rattled.

Max stopped, turned, and looked toward the abrupt noise.

The old man kept from muttering a single word. He stepped farther away from the door, backing deeper into the shadows.

Russell peered through the slanted, white-wooden blinds to the street. He spotted movement on the sidewalk, next to the alley.

Dark Roads

Oh no.

He dropped to the floor in a blink and took cover behind one of the desks nearby.

Max moved to his side, then laid flat on his belly at Russell's boots.

Russell craned his neck, looking over the top of the desk at the window.

A shadow traced across the office, then stopped.

Max licked at his fingers. He groaned while looking up at Russell.

Russell rubbed the crown of Max's head, then placed his finger against his lips and shushed him.

The doorknob twisted.

The gears and levers inside the brass knob popped and creaked.

The shadow turned around, then headed back the direction it came from.

Russell let out a sigh of relief. He waited a few minutes, stood from behind the desk, then walked toward the windows.

"Are they gone?" the old man asked in a loud whisper from across the room.

"Not sure." Russell peered through the dirt-covered blinds, scanning the street for the black SUV or the men on foot. "Where's your car? I don't see a vehicle parked in front of your office."

"At home in my garage." He walked from the back toward Russell, slow and cautious. "Why? You wanting to rob me of my vehicle or something?"

Russell rolled his eyes. "No. Just wondering is all. I have no interest in your car, or anything else that you have. It's not safe out here with folks breaking into stores and looting."

"You mean like what you're doing?" the old man asked in a condescending tone.

"No. Not the same thing," Russell shot back. "If I acted like those guys out there, our encounter would've gone down very differently, so I'd say that you're lucky that you got me instead of them."

The old man groused, then crossed his arms. He checked the time on his watch.

Russell scanned over the streets for another ten minutes or so, finding it to be free and clear of any threats that could be seen from his vantage point.

Max sat on his haunches, waiting for his handler's next command.

They needed to move. Cathy relied on Russell, and he couldn't waste any more time lurking in the shadows.

"Come on, boy." Russell turned away from the window and walked toward the back of the office. Max stood and followed, trotting at his side. "I am sorry for barging in here and any inconvenience this may have caused you. I do appreciate your patience and help."

"Seeing that you barged in with that revolver in hand and a large dog, I didn't have much choice," he replied, cold and callous. "Now, if you'd please leave my business, I would appreciate that."

At least you didn't get robbed or killed. Those people out there wouldn't have been as generous.

Russell kept his mouth sealed. He nodded and walked toward the side entrance of the building. He placed his ear against the door, listening for any signs of movement outside. None could be heard.

Max stood at the ready, facing the opening. The subtle outline of his body moved in the dimness.

Dark Roads

Russell unlocked the door, then cracked it open. Sunlight breached the narrow gap.

Max waited for his orders, probing the air.

He nudged the anxious German shepherd with his leg, moving him off to the side and away from the door. The revolver sat firm in his hand, fingers tightening over the grip as he peered out into the alley. For now, it seemed as though they had given their pursuers the slip.

"All right, let's go." Russell slipped out from the building with Max at his side.

The old man offered no parting words. Instead, he shut the door behind Russell and secured the deadbolt.

Russel and Max skulked along the side of the brick building toward the street. Russell scanned for any movement, listening for the slightest sound.

The wind picked up, gusting hard one minute then settling the next. Lose trash skipped along the pavement past them.

Russell toed the corner of the building, then craned his neck down the road. He spotted the gas station's pylon sign, then a portion of the building, but couldn't see much more than that.

He peered around the edge of the structure, looking in the opposite direction for any inbound vehicles. The street sat empty, void of any cars.

Move fast, stay low. Russell bolted around the corner of the building and sprinted across the street. His boots hammered the road as the go bag shifted about on his shoulders.

Max matched him stride for stride, staying at his side.

They hit the other side of the four-lane road and ran through the parking lot of the donut shop. Concrete turned to grass as they kept out of sight from the main road.

Russell slowed to catch his breath. His hands rested on his hips as he gasped for air. He kept moving in the direction of the gas station.

Erin crossed his mind. He hoped he had done enough to allow her to get away and find some help.

Billet's came into view. A scant few cars lined the outer edge of the business's parking lot. The vehicles looked empty. He spotted no movement around the side or back of the building, but couldn't see the front from where they stood.

Russell pressed on, moving through the grass and up the slight incline to the parking lot.

Max stayed glued to his side, mimicking his every move.

They slithered down the passenger side of the older model sedan.

Russell peered inside the vehicle's grime-covered window, checking for any keys in the ignition or on the seat. The interior looked in dire shape, the seats ripped and torn. Dust covered the dash and wires dangled from under the steering column.

Max sniffed the ground, then the flat back tire. He lifted his leg and pissed on the rusted rim.

My thoughts exactly.

Russell grabbed Max by the collar and tugged. "Whoa. Watch out for the busted plastic there."

The taillight's covering had been damaged. Shards of the broken pieces lay scattered over the pavement.

Max studied the jagged fragments, sniffing the area.

Russell skirted the plastic and ran for the station. They kept to the back of the building, slipping past the dumpster and stacks of tires. He checked the lone door, testing the silver handle, hoping it would be unlocked.

The handle didn't budge.

Dark Roads

Russell scanned over the ground, searching for anything he might be able to use to pry it open. Nothing caught his attention.

Crap.

"Guess we're trying the front, then." Russell backtracked, then moved around to the front of the building. The lot had a few more cars parked on the far side. He surveyed the grounds, then moved down the walkway toward the entrance.

The gas pumps sat lifeless, the digital readouts blank and gray.

Newspapers flapped from the interior of the open, weathered, blue steel stand next to the ice maker. The wrinkled and smudged ink distorted the latest news that covered the front page.

Max sniffed the few bundles left and moved on.

Russell peeked through the open area between the Marlboro window clings and other marketing material plastered over the glass. Darkness loomed large within the station. He skimmed for any movement, not wanting to be surprised by anyone lurking in the shadows.

It looked clear. No black clad figures caught his eye, though, that didn't mean too much.

He tested the door handle. The door opened with ease. A bell rung from overtop the entrance.

Russell froze, then listened for a response.

Silence lingered, except for the whistling of the wind blowing through the cracked door.

The jamb had been damaged near the lock, the paint scuffed and bent inward.

Russell dipped inside the store with Max trotting past him.

The numerous windows lining the storefront allowed the sun to provide some light, giving Russell a general layout of the building.

191

On the far wall, more windows revealed the shop and the vehicles parked within.

Coolant, coolant, coolant, he thought while walking the narrow aisles.

The racks of various sweets and other odds and ends had been picked through. Discarded wrappers laid on the floor. Unwanted food crunched under his boots, clinging between the grooves. A handful of brass shell casings on the floor caught the light.

He hadn't spotted any dead bodies within the mess, but he hadn't checked the entire building.

Russell moved around the rack toward the back corner of the store and spotted a door that led out to the garage. A bleak four-foot section of automotive products sat next to the entrance.

The shelves sat in disarray. Bottles of engine oil and windshield wiper fluid laid on their sides and on the floor near the base. A number of the containers had rounded holes or slits punched through the labels.

Max studied the puddles of fluids pooled on the floor. His nose crinkled in disgust. He turned away from the mess.

"Who knew trying to find some coolant would be such a pain in the butt," Russell said, mumbling to himself. "We'll check the garage, and if there's not any out there, we'll need to just cut our losses and get back."

Max skirted the wet spot on the floor and waited by the glass door.

Russell stepped over the spill, grabbed the handle, and pulled the door toward him. The hinges squeaked in the silence. No footfalls responded to the noise.

The smell of grease tainted the stagnant air among other unfamiliar scents that assaulted his nose. Light shone through the small, narrow windows molded within the roll-up bay doors.

Dark Roads

A light-brown minivan hung in the air, held up only by the hydraulic two-post lift that ran under its undercarriage. On the far side of the garage, he spotted a four-door truck parked in the stall.

A shimmer of light shone through the windows in the bay doors.

Russell turned and squinted, looking through the smudged plastic to the parking lot of the station.

The bell from inside the store pinged–faint but loud enough to tickle his ear. Movement in his peripheral vision caught his eye.

Russell stooped down, then made for the cinderblock wall below the windows. "Max, come here."

The German shepherd rushed to his side, looking at him with ears perked–waiting for his command.

Russell stood, then peered over the edge of the wall through the window. They were no longer alone.

CHAPTER TWENTY

SARAH

T he air blasted from the vents of the sedan, brushing against Sarah's flushed, tacky skin. Tiny bumps populated her forearms and chest. She thumbed the dial to the coldest setting, dropping the inside temperature of the hitman's ride to an artic level.

A musty scent filled her nose, mixing with the palpable stench of cheap cologne and cigars. It churned her stomach, knowing the vile men had been there to steal her away and that they scoured the city searching for her.

An engine backfired from the car she passed at full speed. Sarah flinched. Her nerves were racked and frayed beyond comprehension. She gripped the tan steering wheel tighter, turning her knuckles and fingers a milky white.

Sarah pulled in front of the small red hatchback and kept her foot mashed to the floorboard.

Dark Roads

The streets had few cars running through the city. Portions of the roads had been blocked off with police barricades or vehicles. The random fires burning from transformers blowing or any other number of reasons had been snuffed out.

The palm of her hand rubbed over her face. She blinked, then shook her head. Focusing on the road ahead proved to be a challenge in her sleep-deprived state.

Sarah breathed deep, held, then released the pent-up tension and stress through pursed lips. Her mind worked nonstop.

The reel of torture and death seemed endless, flooding her mind and drowning her thoughts in a sea of hurt and pain that wouldn't let up. Being strong took courage, but it also took energy— something she lacked.

Sarah blew through the intersection without braking. She offered a half-hearted glance down either side of the street for any inbound vehicles. Her home was on the next block over and she couldn't wait to be inside.

Flashing red and blue lights up ahead jarred Sarah from the distracting thoughts that raced through her mind. The Boston police cruiser flew past her at full tilt with its siren blaring.

Sarah turned onto her street and sped toward her home. She skimmed over the nearby houses for any strange men lurking about—or Spencer for that matter.

The deviant knew where she lived and that troubled Sarah, despite the fact that he had saved her twice. He had to be up to something, plotting some sort of ploy to gain her trust.

Sarah pulled along the curb in front of her home, then shifted the sedan into park. She scanned the windows and door of her two-bedroom abode, looking for any signs of a break or hint of trouble waiting for her inside.

All looked just as she had left it a few days ago.

The idling engine grumbled. Sarah turned the AC off, then killed the engine. She removed the keys and slung open the door.

The air outside didn't feel as good as the brisk touch of the manufactured coldness of the vehicle's system.

Mrs. Greenwood peeked from her window at the unfamiliar car from the safety of her home across the street. Sarah spotted her white nightgown and one of her many cats strutting in the front windowsill of her Pepto-Bismol colored home. She had a knack for watching the neighborhood for any strange happenings.

Sarah offered the widow a nod and a subtle wave.

Mrs. Greenwood stepped away from the window and closed her blinds without acknowledging the gesture. The cat stared at Sarah for a second longer before licking its private area.

The keys to the sedan dangled from Sarah's fingers. She skirted the front end of the vehicle and walked up her driveway past her truck.

Sarah wished her ride worked as she'd much rather have her own vehicle than that of the hitmen, but it sat dead in her driveway.

She followed the walkway to her front door, then reached for her purse–only to remember that it had been taken from her.

Great.

She tried to figure out a way inside her home that didn't involve busting out a window. A heavy sigh fled her lips as she looked at the front door. She ran her hand over her face in frustration.

I guess if I need to bust a window out, then– A light flickered inside her head–one that gave her hope and worried her at the same time.

She backed away from the door and stopped at the two large bushes planted in front of her house. She glanced to the road and across the street–scanning for any prying eyes.

Dark Roads

A small white stone sat buried in the dirt at the base of the house–concealed by the foliage that grew around it. Sarah bent down, grabbed the stone, and twisted.

The top popped off–revealing a key that she had put there right after she moved in. She had forgotten it about, seeing as it had never been used.

Sarah grabbed the key, secured the stone in place, and walked toward the door. She slipped the end inside the deadbolt, and turned. The lock clicked.

The sound of an approaching vehicle caught her ear. She peered over her shoulder, watching as the SUV rolled past her home without stopping or slowing.

Home sweet home. That's all Sarah could think while twisting the doorknob and walking inside. She slammed the door shut, then leaned against it.

A deep sigh fled her lips. The tension in her shoulders, neck, and back mounted and refused to give her a break. Her hand massaged the back of her head, then her shoulders. It did little good to relieve the pain.

Sarah pushed away from the door, pocketed the house key, and moved through the dim home to the kitchen. She skimmed over the dark hallway, searching for any figures or sounds of movement. Silence filled her ears—the kind that made the fine hairs on one's arms stand on end.

The planks of wood creaked with each step, tightening her nerves a bit more. The keys slipped between her fingers, the pointed tips poking out beyond each digit. She balled her hand into a fist, ready to punish any threat that lurked inside her home.

Light from the bay window in her dining room shone through the blinds. She spotted no movement in her back yard.

Sarah tilted her head to the side, then peeked around the jamb that led into the kitchen. The blinds covering the far window and the one above the sink flooded the small space with sunlight, offering a better sense of her surroundings.

The wind chime dangling outside the window above the sink pinged. A dog barking added to the melody.

A noise from the other end of the home sent Sarah turning about on her heels with her fists up in front of her. It sounded like scratching.

The knife block on the counter sat but a foot or so from her reach.

Sarah dropped the keys to the countertop and grabbed the butcher's knife. The handle felt good in her grasp; much better than the meager set of keys.

She gulped and made her way out of the kitchen and through the dining room.

The hallway leading back to the bedrooms and bathroom sat in a pool of black. Her fingers repositioned over the knife handle, acting as though her grip on the large blade wasn't tight enough.

Sarah moved through the dimness, one slow, precarious step at a time. The thumping of her heart pressing against her chest pulsated in her ear. A tingling sensation washed over her body from the flood of adrenaline that spiked through her veins.

The unsettling feeling of eyes watching her or some sort of threat lurking in her home wouldn't leave her be. All seemed well with no signs or hints of a break-in, but she couldn't help it.

The floor under her feet continued to signal her whereabouts. She cringed from each subtle give of the wood and cussed under her breath. Her mind conjured up a slew of scenarios of masked men waiting under her bed, in a closet, or some other hiding place, ready to attack in her safe space.

Dark Roads

Sarah checked each room and found no evidence of an intruder. The strange sound that tightened her nerves remained a mystery–one that she couldn't explain. Staying in her home by herself seemed like a poor idea given all she had learned and the lengths the people after her would go through, but where could she go?

Tim's place popped inside her head–the last safe haven she could think of. Maybe Tim and Russell had made it back from their trip and had been looking for her.

She craved one of Russell's tight hugs more than anything in the world, and for him to hold her close, so she could feel the warmth of his body and the beating of his heart.

Sarah raced around the bedframe and opened the blinds a hair more to lighten the dark room.

The messy sheets on her bed and the clothes hanging from the open dresser drawers filled her gaze. She ignored the unkept mess and got to work.

Sarah rushed to her closet and threw open the door. She felt along the top shelf, searching for her travel bag. She wanted to pack light, just the essentials to get her through a few days.

The tips of her fingers brushed over a blanket, pillow, then a stack of shoe boxes.

Where the hell is it? Sarah thought, aggravated by the inconvenience. Leaving without some fresh clothes and other items didn't sit well with her. She needed out of the smirched rags that had grown crusty and stiff from days of wear and tear.

Sarah dropped to her knees and rummaged through the contents on the floor. Her hands touched every item, feeling for the bag.

Hold on.

She felt a strap of sorts buried under a mountain of shoes and boots. She grabbed the nylon strand and pulled it from the depths of the cluttered closet into the light, a few pairs of sneakers tumbling to the carpet. She skimmed over the bag, remembering it being bigger, but it would have to do.

A list of items ran through her head as she stood, turned, and headed for the bed. She set the bag on the edge of the crumpled-up sheets and got to work.

Sarah sifted through the drawers of her dresser, yanking out socks, panties, and an additional bra without much thought, and tossed them to her bed. She gathered a few tops and pants from the closet, then crammed them haphazardly into the bag.

She pulled her shirt over her head and threw it at the wall. Her pants stuck to her legs like glue, unwilling to leave her body.

She forced them off her hips and past her sore knees. A slew of bruises populated both legs. The damaged skin had a rainbow of colors–everything from pink and red to blue and dark purple.

The injuries made Sarah shudder as she pulled each pant leg from her body. Standing in the middle of her bedroom, exposed, Sarah caught her reflection in the mirror on top of her dresser. Dried blood clung to her chin and the sides of her cheeks.

Her haggard face and the cuts and scrapes on her upper body made her tear up. She fought to hold it together, not wanting to crumble to pieces.

Sarah grabbed the additional clean clothes from the mattress and rushed to the bathroom. She tossed them onto the counter, then opened the blinds.

The light reflected off the pink tile inside the shower, catching Sarah's eye. The thought of warm water washing away the filth that clung to her flesh gelled in her head, though, she doubted the pressure would be worth the hassle. Instead, she grabbed a wash rag from the drawer in the vanity and settled for a quick sink bath.

Dark Roads

Sarah twisted the knobs on the faucet. A slow, steady dribble of water leaked from the tap. She ran the rag under the thin stream, saturating the wash cloth as much as she could.

The cool water felt good against her hands. She rang the rag out some, then ran the cloth over her face. The coarse fabric scratched her sensitive skin, but Sarah didn't mind the slight annoyance. She scrubbed what she could from her face, then hit other points of interest on her body.

Sarah discarded the rag on the corner of the sink, then fished out her deodorant from the drawer to her right. Each armpit received copious amounts of the odor-blocking white stick.

The person looking back at her in the mirror almost appeared human and not a haggard mess that had seen better days. Almost.

The pampering ended with Sarah dressing in the fresh, clean clothes she pulled from the dresser and closet. She gathered up her dirty under garments and lugged them back to her room–adding them to the pile against the far wall.

Sarah slipped on some sneakers from her closet, then thumbed through the items she'd stuffed in her bag, pondering if she should grab some more.

The wood floor in the hallway creaked a warning in the silence, similar to when she walked over it.

Sarah froze, then looked to the open bedroom door. Fear stole her breath, choking off any words that dared to escape her lips. Her heart thumped harder, faster. The muscles in her arms tightened.

She listened close, making sure her mind hadn't played a trick on her. The subtle sound played again.

Spencer. It has to be him, Sarah thought. He had been to her place before and lurked outside her windows like some crazed killer from those cheesy '80's horror movies. Though, the other hitmen and mobsters could find her just as easily if they wanted to, she imagined.

The movement from the living room grew more apparent— footfalls moving through her home echoed in the silence. She looked to the butcher's knife lying on top of the dresser. It wasn't her Glock 43, but it would have to do.

Sarah moved toward the dresser, slow and silent. Her hands trembled, body quaking with apprehension. Spencer wouldn't leave her thoughts. He wanted her bad and wouldn't relinquish his desire to get her at any cost.

The knife rested against her palm. Her fingers closed over the thick steel handle. She flipped the knife around with the razor-sharp blade facing the floor.

Sarah toed the transition strip, then peered out into the hallway. A shadow played over the far wall from the living room. Her stomach twisted in knots as she gripped the knife even tighter.

Another set of footfalls sounded from the kitchen along with the opening and closing of cabinets.

She slipped around the jamb out into the hallway. Her body clung to the wall as she stalked the intruders who had invaded her sanctuary.

The hammering of her heart grew more intense the closer she got. She worried the men would hear her panic, smell her fear.

A figure came into view just past the edge of the wall in the hallway. A sliver of its arm and the gun clutched in its hand caught her eye.

Sarah took a deep breath, held it, then lunged from the blackness of the hallway.

The figure turned to face her as she slashed up at an angle with the butcher's knife. The blade sliced through his long-sleeve dark blue shirt. He stumbled backward, tripping over his feet to avoid being stabbed.

Dark Roads

Sarah stayed on the offensive, charging the frantic man who waved his Glock 22 from the flat of his back.

"Wait, don't fire," a raspy voice said from the far side of the dining room. He ran toward her with his hands in the air, his Glock 22 trained at the ceiling.

Sarah stopped dead in her tracks, then cut her eyes over to the suit that stood at the edge of her table. That's when it hit her like a lightning bolt. They were Boston PD.

"Sarah, can you please lower the knife and stand down?" the suit asked, calm and nonthreatening.

He looked familiar, but she couldn't place a name with his bearded, aged face. The beat cop lying flat on his back also looked familiar. Her mind worked, looking at both men until the suit's name popped inside her head. "Detective Stone?"

Derek Shupert

CHAPTER TWENTY-ONE

SARAH

Sarah lowered the butcher knife, but kept a firm grip around the handle. She took a step back from the cop who held her at gun point with his Glock 22.

"What the hell are you doing inside my home?" she asked, perturbed by the men skulking about her place. "I could've killed either of you, or you could've shot me."

Stone lowered his arms, then nodded at the cop on the floor. "Renner, lower your firearm. Let's all take a deep breath here and just relax, okay?"

Renner removed his finger from the trigger guard, then diverted the Glock 22 away from her. He sat up straight, then got his legs under him.

Sarah eyed both men, wondering why they stood in her home. "How did you get inside? I thought I locked the door behind me?"

"The front door was unlocked. We spotted the strange car at the curb, and thought something might be wrong." Stone secured the Glock in the holster inside his sports jacket. Renner slid his sidearm into the holster fixed to his duty belt. "We didn't mean to startle you."

"Well, you failed at that." Sarah took a deep breath, trying to come down from the rush. Her chest heaved with excitement—fingers tingling.

She knew Detective Stone from when he worked Jess's murder case. He did an okay job, though she felt he could've done more. David stepped in and helped as he could under the radar, not wanting to undermine the detective or his commanding officers' orders to stand down and leave it be.

"So, you're okay, then?" Stone asked, glancing down the hallway toward her bedroom. "There isn't anyone else here with you, is there? Wouldn't want any more surprises."

Sarah shook her head. "No. It's just me."

"Good. We're glad you're safe, then." Stone walked toward her. Her stranglehold on the butcher's knife remained taut. He stopped, lifting his hands back up in protest. "Whoa. Easy. We're the good guys, here. You can put down the knife, Sarah."

Something didn't add up. "How did you know something happened to me?"

Stone glanced at Renner, then said, "David."

Sarah's jaw dropped. How could that be? David was dead. "David's... alive?"

"Yes. He's pretty banged up, but he's still with us," Stone answered.

Dark Roads

A flood of emotions slammed into Sarah like a tidal wave. She couldn't believe Vin, Kinnerk's hitman for higher who kidnapped her and Mandy, didn't kill David.

"David radioed the station asking for assistance. A nearby unit arrived on the scene, and found him outside on the curb next to his patrol car, shot twice in his chest. Bastard is lucky to be alive, that's for sure." Stone lowered his arms once more, but kept his distance. "He said that someone attacked the both of you when entering your friend's apartment."

Renner moved toward the front door of her home, then peered out through the window. His one hand rested on his hip while the other caressed the grip of the holstered Glock. He glanced back to Sarah, then over to Stone.

"Is your arm all right?" Sarah asked, looking at the torn fabric of his long-sleeve, dark-blue, button-up shirt. "I hope it's not too bad of a cut."

"Yeah. The cut isn't that deep. I'll get it looked at later," Renner replied, staring back out the window of the door.

Sarah looked over at Stone. "Is there any way I can see David? I want him to know that I'm okay?"

He shook his head. "We need to get you to safety first, but you'll be able to soon. For now, I'd like for you to come with us down to the station, so we can go over what happened. Get a statement, and see if we can puzzle this together. Right now, you're our only lead."

The lingering feeling of something being wrong with the two cops in her house wouldn't leave Sarah alone. The odd glances they shot one another and the way Renner stood by her front door, almost blocking it with his wide frame, grinded on her mind.

Why are they looking at each other like that and acting strange? Sarah thought, watching the two officers with keen eyes. *Perhaps I need to calm down and relax.*

Sarah knew the detective some, and they both wore the Boston PD shield, after all. Why would they want to hurt her?

"Um, yeah. Sure." Sarah pointed at the hallway. "I'm going to grab my bag from the other room first."

Stone held out his arm. "Yeah, sure. Grab what you need, then we'll leave."

Renner remained stationed at the door, like a sentry on watch.

Sarah set the butcher knife on the top of her entertainment center, then walked down the hallway.

Stone fell in line behind her. He kept but a few paces back, not leaving much distance between them.

"You know, you can wait in the other room. I doubt anyone is going to try anything with a police cruiser out front," Sarah said, entering her bedroom.

"One can't be too careful or underestimate the lengths these sorts of individuals will go to," Stone responded, leaning on the jamb with his arms folded across his chest. "Look at all the craziness that's happened since the blackout. We've descended into chaos, and it's only getting worse."

Sarah nodded from the foot of her bed, checking the contents one last time inside her bag. "That is true. This event has shown the dark side of humanity. I never thought I'd see the day that anything like this would ever happen."

Stone watched her every move, then checked the time on his watch. "Yeah. The mayor has called in the National Guard to give us a hand in restoring order. They're assessing the situation. There's also a curfew that'll be put into effect soon. Lock the city down tight.

People won't be happy about it, but it needs to be done to cull the chaos."

"If it helps stops all of the rioting and other bad things people are doing, I guess it'll be good," Sarah replied.

"That's the goal." Stone shifted his weight between his legs, then checked the time again on his watch. He seemed antsy, distracted even. "You know, you're pretty lucky to have survived and escaped from those men. They're dangerous and most aren't as fortunate."

Sarah paused with her hand wrapped about the black straps of her travel bag. *I didn't say how many.* That eerie feeling blossomed into sudden panic. "Yeah. Lucky. Um, how did you know there was more than one man involved and how dangerous they are?"

Stone cleared his throat, then diverted his gaze for a moment. "David told us that the two of you encountered multiple hostiles inside that apartment. We can go over all the other details and your statement at the station, but we really need to be going."

"Yes. Of course. I understand." Sarah offered a warm smile even though the budding fear coalescing inside of her grew to a volcanic state. Sarah pointed at the far end of the dresser in the corner of her bedroom. "Could you do me a favor and see if you can find my wallet over there? I seem to have misplaced it."

Stone pushed away from the jamb, sighed, then smiled. "Sure." He looked over the top of the dresser, then down at the floor.

Sarah walked toward the edge of her bed in the direction of the nightstand nestled in the corner, then stopped. She turned back around and grabbed the handle of her bag.

"I'm not seeing it anywhere," Stone said, with his back to her.

"It has to be here somewhere." Sarah swung the bag as hard as she could as Stone turned to face her.

The side of the bag slammed into his head. A faint yelp escaped his bearded mouth, followed by a low growl. He stumbled backward into her dresser, knocking it hard against the wall. One hand palmed his skull, the other dug inside the flap of his jacket for the Glock.

"Ah, damnit," he moaned through his clenched jaw, leaning against the dense piece of furniture.

Sarah punched him in the face, then shoved him to the floor–adding insult to injury.

Detective Stone writhed on the floor, palming his face as he fumbled the Glock from its holster. He yelled for his partner from the flat of his back. "Renner."

The cop rushed toward the hallway, his footfalls hammering the wooden floor.

Sarah ran out of her bedroom at full tilt and met the officer in the dark hallway. The outline of his wide frame consumed most of the narrow hall, blocking her path.

Renner pulled his gun from the holster, then brought it to bear. His finger slipped inside the trigger guard and squeezed.

Sarah swung the travel bag at the dark mass before her–knocking his arms toward the wall.

The Glock barked.

A brief flash of orange flared as the sharp report made her ears ring.

"Christ. Don't shoot her, you idiot," Stone yelled from her bedroom. "They want her alive."

Sarah pressed the cop against the wall and tried to move past him.

Renner dipped his shoulder and shoved backward–putting some distance between them. "Stop resisting or I'll make you."

Dark Roads

"Resist this." Sarah lunged forward, grabbed him by the tops of his shoulders, and drove her knee deep into his groin.

The cop doubled over, dropped his Glock to the floor, and lurched forward, grasping his genitals.

Sarah pushed her way past him and headed for the front door. Her hands worked to unlock the deadbolt and chain that ran from the wall to the door.

"Get her," Stone shouted from the hallway.

Crap. Sarah retreated from the front door and ran toward the dining room.

Stone staggered from the hallway and reached for Sarah's arm. "There's nowhere to go, Sarah. You might as well stop running."

"Screw you." Sarah slipped through his fingers with ease and rushed into the kitchen. She skirted the edge of the counter and ran for the back door.

A single deadbolt stood between her and a chance to get away from the corrupt cops.

She flipped the brass lock, grabbed the doorknob, and twisted as footfalls stalked her from the far side of the kitchen.

Detective Stone fumbled his way through the kitchen. He skirted the corner of the counter and lurched toward her.

Sarah flung open the door and darted out of the house.

Stone grabbed the tips of her hair and jerked.

Her head snapped back, but her legs kept moving forward. Sarah shrieked. She yanked her head forward, ripping the strands of her dirty hair from the detective's hand.

"Get the car and head around back to the alley," he said, to his partner. "She's on foot. I'm going to pursue."

Sarah tightened her grip over the handles of the travel bag–sprinting as fast as her sore ankle would allow over the concrete walkway.

The back of the privacy fence that encompassed her small, but quaint backyard had a gate that led out into the alley. The latch had given her problems for some time. She hoped it would cooperate.

Sarah checked over her shoulder, nearing the gate.

Stone lumbered down the walkway, struggling to keep up with her. His gut and double chin jiggled from the exertion. Sweat raced from his receding hairline and down his plump cheeks.

The travel bag clutched in her hand swung to and fro in her arms.

Sarah grabbed the black handle of the gate and jerked it to the side. It didn't budge. "Come on. Give me a break here." She fought it a moment more before letting go.

Stone picked up the pace, lugging his rounded body through the ankle-high grass.

Forget it. Sarah tossed her bag over the six-and-a-half-foot tall fence, then scaled the cross beams.

The fence swayed from her weight. The rotted dog-eared planks cracked and gave as she pulled on the tips of them.

Stone grabbed the back of her jeans and pulled.

"Get your hands off me." Sarah kicked her leg at the detective, striking him in the chest.

He released her pants.

Sarah climbed over the top and dropped to the ground. Her ankle gave on impact, sending her to the weeds.

The Boston police cruiser came to a skidding halt over the rocky alleyway. Flashing lights loomed from the top of the car.

The gate rattled in place as Stone yelled out. "You better knab her."

Dark Roads

Sarah peeled herself from the dirt and scooped up her bag. She limped past the cruiser in the opposite direction.

Renner emerged from the driver's seat and raced toward the back of the vehicle. The shot to his manhood hindered his movements some, but not enough. He gained on Sarah fast, and tackled her.

They hit the ground hard. Her bag flew from her hand. The much larger cop straddled her waist and pinned her arms to the itchy weeds.

Stone worked his way through the gate and lumbered past the cruiser. His chest heaved from the chase. He bent over with the heels of his palms resting on the soft parts just above his knees as he tried to catch his breath. "Get her in the cruiser, now."

"No. Please don't do this," Sarah said, pleading with the cops while trying to free her arms. "Just let me go. No one will know."

Renner stood and wrenched her off the ground. He pulled her arms behind her back and handcuffed her.

Stone took a deep breath, then exhaled. "I'm sorry, but we can't do that. You're not the only one under the gun here."

Renner escorted Sarah to the cruiser, dumping her into the back seat.

Stone retrieved her bag from the ground, then tossed it into the back with her. He slammed the door shut and got into the front passenger seat. Renner took the driver's side and closed his door.

Sarah sat up from the seat and peered out the window, wondering what ill-fate awaited her now.

CHAPTER TWENTY-TWO

RUSSELL

The armed men searched the store, riffling through every section for their mark. They didn't seem concerned with being silent.

Russell counted three hostiles–all armed. He captured quick glances of their hands and pistols wedged inside their gloved palms.

Max couldn't see the threat, but he played off Russell's tense posture and stress-filled sighs. The German shepherd shifted his weight between his front paws, then groaned.

"Yeah. We're in a bad spot here," Russell said, dipping below the window. "They must've spotted us moving this way."

Loud crashes and bangs echoed around them. Max stood from his haunches and growled.

Russell rubbed the top of his head between his ears, trying to calm him down and keep him from giving up their position.

Dark Roads

A beam of light shone through the glass from inside the station.

Russell moved away from the wall, but stopped, catching sight of the light tracing over the rear tire of the van loaded on the two-pole hydraulic lift. It moved about the space like a spotlight, searching for any movement. He kept a tight hold around Max's neck, waiting for the chance to move.

The light shifted toward the back wall of the garage, illuminating the various sized tool chests and other machinery nestled between the large, red, steel containers.

Russell scrambled from the cinderblock wall with Max at his side. The duo moved past the rear of the lifted van and a stack of tires next to the vehicle. He took a quick peek out into the parking lot from the windows inside the bay doors and spotted a vehicle parked out front. It looked like the black SUV.

The door leading into the garage from the station opened. The hinges squeaked a warning in the deafening silence.

"They've got to be here somewhere," a voice said, shouting from inside the station. "They headed this way. We tear this place apart until we find them. They've gotten a good look at us."

Russell skirted the tailgate of the four-door Chevy pickup and hid on the passenger side of the vehicle. His back pressed against the body of the truck, eyes focused on the workbench before him. He took a deep breath, formulating his play.

Max paced the concrete floor, then trotted toward the front end of the pickup. His dark brown and black coat melded with the dimness of the garage, concealing his body some. He waited at the corner of the bumper, then peered around toward the other end of the shop.

Lights traced over the floor, walls, and through the windows of the cab of the pickup they took refuge behind. Footsteps filled

Russell's ears. Two men from what he could tell. They moved like bulls in a china shop, loud and unabated.

Max growled louder the closer they got. He inched past the bumper of the pickup.

"Max, no," Russell said, in a whisper, reaching for the canine.

The German shepherd took off in a dead sprint, barking and growling.

"Oh, Christ," one of the men yelled.

A sharp report echoed inside the garage, followed by screams of panic.

Russell bolted from the side of the pickup and grabbed a wrench from the edge of the workbench before him.

The weighted steel felt good in his palm as he ran around the front of the pickup truck.

Max had one of the men down on the ground, biting at any portion of his flailing body he could sink his fangs into. The flashlight's beam trained at the pickup truck at the man's side as he kicked his legs and fought to keep Max at bay.

An orange flash of light lit up the bay doors. Another sharp report battered the enclosed garage.

Russell flinched, ducked, then covered his head. He pulled the trigger on instinct. The revolver barked, discharging its final round.

Max kept the pressure on the man prone on his back, clawing and fighting for any piece he could snag. He took a boot to the side of his head, ripping a yelp from his maw.

Oh, no you didn't hit my dog. Russell thought, worried and angered by the cry from his companion.

The man pointed his gun at Max and squeezed the trigger.

Russell swung the hefty wrench, striking his wrist.

"Ahh." The pistol fired, then fell from his trembling hands.

Dark Roads

The round missed Max by a mile and punched the cinderblock wall above the tool boxes.

A wave of emotions overtook Russell as he struck the defenseless man with the wrench. He continued to swing his arm without pause, pounding the man's face and any other part of his body he could find.

Light shone from behind Russell. The hastened footfalls rushed toward him.

Max growled and attacked.

Something dense smashed into the back of Russell's skull, scrambling his brain. His vision blurred, and the world spun out of control. He dumped over to his side onto the floor.

"Jesus Christ," a raspy voice said, towering over Russell. "He smashed Jimmy's face in with a damn wrench."

The strident light blasted Russell in the face, sealing his lids tight.

"Get that mutt under control," the man standing in front of Russell said, in a hoarse tone. "We'll see what the boss wants to do with it."

Max yelped again, then grew silent.

They dragged Russell's body across the garage floor and out through the bay door. The point of impact on the back of his skull radiated pain. He opened his eyes to a blurred world and bright sunlight that caused his lids to clamp shut once more.

They stripped his pack from his back, then dropped his arms to the concrete. He gritted his teeth against the pain and felt the back of his head, probing the sore spot.

Max continued barking and growling. Another yelp sounded, followed by a dense thud hitting the ground.

"Get that dog secured pronto." The man's voice sounded familiar. The man from the drug store. He must be their leader. "I

217

told you that you wouldn't get too far and you'd regret crossing us, hero. Just who the hell are you exactly?"

Russell rolled to his side, then to his hands and knees. He grumbled while cupping the back of his head. "Nobody. Just passing through is all. Looking for some supplies."

"You don't seem like a nobody to me," the man replied. "Not many folks in town would do what you did. Then again, most are staying home because of the blackout. Temporary orders from the police, who at the moment, are swamped with various calls giving us open range on the businesses, and you are messing up our time table."

"He killed Jimmy, Ty. Beat him to death with a damn wrench." One of the men standing watch behind Russell shoved him in the back, pushing him to the pavement.

Russell pressed his hands to the concrete, preventing himself from smacking the pavement face first. "He shot at my dog then hit him. To be fair, none of this would've happened if you would've just let us be. What went down in that garage is on your head. Not mine."

The barrel of a pistol pressed against the sore spot on the back of Russell's skull. "Let me pop him right here, Ty, so we can finish what we started and head out before the cops show back up. Time's a ticking and this asshole is messing with our money."

The crackling of a radio sounded from Ty's belt, followed by another familiar voice that spoke through the static.

"Ty, you there? Come over, will ya?" John Deere said.

Ty pointed to Barry, then said, "Hold on. Don't do anything yet."

"But-"

"Watch him and do not pull that damn trigger until I say otherwise." Ty paused, then said. "Yeah. What is it? We're in a bit of a situation here. Make it quick."

Dark Roads

Russell kept his head pointed at the ground. His blurred vision waned, bringing color to his blood-stained hands.

"We got a bead on those two who attacked us at the gas station," John Deere said, over the radio. "We spotted their Bronco at some old abandoned house off the highway."

Cathy. Damn it.

Ty paced about in front of Russell, listening to the hillbilly who had threatened them the day before.

Russell tilted his head far enough to gauge the strength of the crew surrounding him and to locate Max. Aside from Ty and Barry, he counted two other men standing near the black SUV.

Max laid on his side, tied to the hitch at the back.

"I thought I told you to drop that and handle business. Our payday is more important than some damn grudge against some chick, guy, and his–" Ty stopped speaking and moving.

"Listen. That damn German shepherd mauled my arm, and they nearly killed us," John Deere said, pleading his case.

"German shepherd, huh?" Ty asked.

"Yeah. Damn thing clamped down on me, and didn't want to let go," John Deere answered.

"You're looking at the house right now?" Ty asked, his muddy boots pointed in Russell's direction.

"We are. We're back a ways on the gravel road. Almost missed it," John Deere replied.

"Good. Stay put and keep an eye on the place. Don't do anything until we get there."

"Copy that."

The radio clicked, then fell silent.

Russell's mind raced. A flood of panic surged through his body. Ty had him bent over a barrel and Cathy at the mercy of the two sick hillbillies who wanted nothing more than to violate her.

"Man, you're just all over the place trying to muck up my business, aren't you?" Ty stepped toward Russell, then stooped down. He lifted Russell's head up with the business end of his pistol.

"Like I said, we're just passing through and stopped for supplies. They started it, and well, we did what we had to do. We don't want any trouble. Just let us be on our way, and you and your crew can do whatever. Not our business," Russell answered, staring at the chiseled chin and five o'clock shadow of the dark-haired man.

"Not your business, huh? It sure didn't seem that way back in that drug store. You made it your business in there." Ty removed the pistol from under Russell's chin, then stood back up. "After all, we can't let you or that woman off. That wouldn't be good for my business.

Russell sat up straight on his knees, then flitted his gaze to Ty. He didn't want to die on his knees, but what else could he do to stop it?

Ty adjusted his grip over the piece, training the barrel at the middle of Russell's forehead. "Time for us to conclude our business here, hero. I'll give your regards to your lady friend."

Dark Roads

CHAPTER TWENTY-THREE

RUSSELL

Ty loomed over Russell like a vengeful God who had passed judgement on a mere peasant. Russell had no other play. His fate had been sealed.

Ty's men stood near the SUV, watching and waiting for the job to be done. Black Mustache looked at Russell with a wicked smirk, acting like murdering a man on his knees provided good entertainment.

I'm sorry I couldn't make it back to you, baby. I tried my hardest. Please forgive me, Russell thought.

A crackle of thunder rumbled in the distance. It took a second for the noise to register in his head.

Black Mustache's body twisted away from the front end of the SUV and fell to the concrete, blood spattering over the surface. "Ah, my shoulder."

222

Ty flinched, ducked, then turned his back to Russell, searching for the location of the shooter. "Who the hell is shooting at us?"

"I don't know," Barry shouted.

Russell covered his head, unsure what to do in the chaos.

Another crackle sounded off, followed by Barry screaming in pain.

A thud hit the ground behind Russell, followed by wails of pain and agony.

"Everyone, get in the SUV, now," Ty said, helping Black Mustache off the pavement.

Max stood on all fours, pulling at the rope around his neck that attached to the hitch.

Russell turned around and spotted Barry prone on his back, clutching the side of his young-looking face. Blood seeped out from between his fingers and ran down the back of his hand.

The gun he carried sat on the ground next to him. His free hand felt the ground near his side–fingers searching for the weapon.

Incoming gunfire pinged off the SUV and pelted the front of the station.

Car doors opened then slammed shut. Russell lunged for the pistol. Barry grabbed the grip, his finger over the trigger. Russell seized his arm and shoved it at the pavement.

The pistol discharged, firing toward the street.

The SUV's engine jumped to life, followed by squealing tires.

Max.

Russell pinned Barry's arm to the ground, then punched him in the face until he yielded. The back of his head bounced off the concrete before his body went limp.

The SUV tore ass out of the station's parking lot and hit the main road. It swerved from side to side as it sped away.

The rope fluttered in the wind from the vehicles hitch, but Russell didn't see his companion in tow.

Russell pried the pistol from Barry's hand, then peered over his shoulder.

Max trotted over to him, favoring his front right leg.

"I'm so glad you're all right. You had me worried there." Russell breathed a bit easier, rubbing the German shepherd's head.

Max leaned into his touch, then licked at his face.

Now who the hell shot at us? Russell looked out across the street for the shooter who saved their lives. Since Ty and his men split, the firing ceased.

A figure lurked around the buildings. He had what appeared to be a rifle in his hands.

Max sniffed Barry's unconscious body, then turned to face the road.

Russell ejected the magazine of the 9mm Smith and Wesson he relieved from Barry and took stock of the ammo inside. He had maybe six rounds to work with.

The man ran across the street with his rifle clutched in both hands.

Max barked and bared his fangs at the approaching stranger.

Russell slapped the magazine back into the well, then cycled a round. He flipped over, placed his finger inside the trigger guard, and trained the 9mm at the man.

"Whoa, there. Take it easy. If I wanted you dead, I could've shot you from back there." The man stopped, then raised his hands.

The bill of his camo hat pulled down over his brow, concealing a portion of his face. He looked stocky from what Russell could tell, although, the green and brown camo jacket made it tough to see.

Dark Roads

Max inched forward, growling and putting himself between Russell and the stranger.

"Who are you?" Russell asked, keeping the 9mm trained at his chest.

"The person who just saved your life." He pointed at the piece. "You mind lowering that and calling your dog off?"

Russell removed his finger from the trigger and placed it on the side of the weapon. "Sorry. We're a bit on edge. It's been a rough, stressful day. Max, it's all right."

Max eased off his aggressive stance, but kept a watchful eye on the stranger.

"You all right?" the man asked, slinging the strap of his rifle over his shoulder.

Russell lowered his weapon. "Yeah. A little banged up, but that's nothing new."

"I'm Clyde." He stepped forward with his hand extended.

Max growled.

"Russell Cage. This is Max." Russell reached out and took his hand.

Clyde pulled him off the pavement, then took a step back. "Protective dog."

Russell glanced at Max who stayed close to him. "He is that for sure."

"How'd you get tangled up with them?" Clyde asked, nodding in the direction the SUV took off.

"Bad luck from the looks of it." Russell spotted his rucksack on the ground close by. "My friend and I ran into them out on the highway a ways back. It didn't go too well. They shot her in the leg, then our vehicle broke down. We had to walk here to find some medical supplies for her and coolant for the truck. That's when we

225

encountered them robbing the drug store up the street, among other businesses shut down because of the blackout."

Clyde nodded as Russell retrieved his pack from the ground. "Yeah. For the past few days, they've been hitting small towns, robbing businesses and causing all sorts of problems for folks. I tracked them to this town. They hurt my wife pretty bad. She… didn't make it."

Russell secured the rucksack over his shoulders, then tightened the strap. "I'm sorry for your loss. I can't imagine how that must feel."

"Like salt in an open wound," Clyde replied.

Hearing the sad tale made Russell fear for Cathy's safety, more than he already had.

Corona and John Deere hinted at wanting to do unspeakable things to her. Cathy could handle herself, but she also had an injury that would hinder her being able to fight and get away.

"My friend is in trouble, and we need to get back to her. You wouldn't happen to have a vehicle close by, would you?" Russell looked upon Clyde's sad and solemn face, hoping he did.

Clyde tugged at the strap of his rifle, jammed his thumb and forefinger into each socket, then pointed in the direction he came from. "Yeah. I've got my truck stashed over near those buildings. They know what it looks like, so I wanted to keep it out of sight."

"Would you mind giving us a ride back? It took a bit to walk here from the place we're holed up in. My friend is there alone, and they already have a few people waiting close by. I'm worried what they'll do to her before we can make it back."

"Yes, of course." Clyde turned toward the street. "Follow me."

Russell took a step forward, paused, then looked at the garage.

"What's wrong?" Clyde asked, looking confused.

Dark Roads

"The damn coolant. I never found any," Russell replied.

"Forget it. I got some in my truck. Let's move." Clyde took off, his boots hammering the pavement with Russell and Max trailing him. They ran across the street at a good clip.

Max favored his front leg, galloping with a slight limp to his stride.

Russell couldn't help but scan over the streets and buildings they passed for any more unwanted surprises.

"We're right up here, just past this storage unit," Clyde said. He skirted the corner of the tan steel building and down the row of units. The front end of a white truck stuck out a hair from the passageway that cut through the small buildings.

Clyde shoved his hand into his coat pocket. The lights on the truck flashed. He moved around the front to the driver's side.

Max lagged behind. His tongue dangled from his mouth, the limping growing worse.

Russell stopped and ran back to him. "I got you, big man." He bent down and scooped the German shepherd from the asphalt.

The truck roared to life, idling smooth and clean. Not a single hiccup or misfire loomed from the beast of a truck.

Clyde settled into the driver's seat as Russell lugged Max toward the pickup. The passenger side window retracted. "Need any help?"

"Naw. I got it. I'm going to put him in the back seat if that's all right," Russell said.

"Of course."

Russell lifted Max into the air, trying to reach the door handle. The German shepherd had some weight to him, testing Russell's strength.

Clyde unlatched his seat belt and opened his door as Russell grabbed the handle and pulled.

A gush of cool air escaped the truck, hitting Russell in the face. He placed Max on the rich brown leather seats and slammed the door shut.

Max sniffed the seats, then plopped down.

Russell climbed into the passenger seat and secured his door.

Clyde latched his seat belt and rolled up the window. He placed the truck into drive and punched the gas.

They barreled out of the nook and booked it down the drive toward the street.

Russell fastened his seat belt, grabbed the bar in the corner of the cab, and held on tight. His mind raced. Cathy filled his thoughts.

What does that sick bastard have in store for her? Russell thought, feeling guilty that his actions caused more problems than not, and that she'd pay the ultimate price.

CHAPTER TWENTY-FOUR

SARAH

Renner cut his eyes to the rear-view mirror, stared at Sarah with an emotionless gaze, then looked back to the road ahead of them. The dead stare sent a chill down her spine and made her that much more worried about her uncertain future.

She sat silent in the back seat of the Boston Police cruiser, devising a way out of the situation she had landed in. Sarah wondered if the cops worked for Kinnerk, Leatherface, or another threat she didn't yet know about.

Stone made the consequences clear if Sarah tried to escape or attract any undue attention to them. They couldn't kill her, but breaking fingers or hobbling a leg among other forms of torture would be implemented.

Sarah took the threat as serious and behaved, for now. She had already dealt the two cops a heaping dose of punishment and feared a swift and brutal response for any further aggressive actions.

The metal bit at her already sore wrists. Any little tug or pull sent a shockwave of pain lancing through her arms and body.

"Were you telling the truth about David?" Sarah asked, slouched in the backseat with her arms secured behind her back. "Can you at least tell me that since you won't tell me where you're taking me?"

Stone turned his head to the side, but didn't look into the backseat of the squad car. "Yes. David is a good cop. I respect and like him. Sucked to see him in that sort of shape."

"He's like family. We've known him for a long time." Sarah looked out the window, watching the buildings and what few people trekked along the sidewalks as they traveled down the street.

"Have you heard from Russell, lately?" Stone asked. "We've been looking for him as well, but haven't been able to find him."

Russell? Why would they ask about him?

"I spoke to him the day the blackout happened. Haven't heard a peep from him since." Saying the words crushed Sarah, but she held it together. "Why do you want to know about him?"

"Did he say where he was heading by chance?" Stone ignored the last part of Sarah's question. He whispered to Renner, then pointed at the intersection.

"Just that he was going out of town. He didn't say where, and I didn't ask." Another regret she had in a laundry list that continued to grow by the second.

"Kind of strange you didn't ask where your husband is going, isn't it? I mean, if my wife was leaving town, I'd at least like to know where she's going," Stone said.

Renner slowed, then rolled through the nonfunctioning intersection. They turned down Peterson Blvd. and continued on.

Dark Roads

"We're separated at the moment, so no, I didn't ask where." Sarah wondered why Stone wanted to know about Russell. What did it mean?

"I imagine you're worried about him, having disappeared like that. Don't worry, though. We'll track him and his friend Tim down." Stone's ominous threat or statement, Sarah didn't know how to take it, hung in the air.

Sarah gulped, fearful for not only her safety, but that of her husband's as well. Sarah hoped Russell fared better than she had.

"Take Amber Lane, then the alley next to Sal's Pizzeria," Stone said.

Renner nodded.

The part of Boston they traveled through looked much the same as the rest of the city Sarah had seen. The widespread chaos and looting had left its mark on the nearby buildings and any cars that lined the streets.

Windows in businesses had been busted out. The exteriors had been tagged with red and black spray paint. Some of the cars they passed showed signs of gunfire. What few people she saw lessened to a deserted block, leaving her alone on the dark road.

Renner braked, then spun the steering wheel clockwise. The cruiser pulled into the narrow alley next to the pizzeria that had been untouched by the madness.

Sarah spotted two black BMW's parked alongside the side entrance of a sprawling brick building. Two bald men, dressed in black sport coats and standing guard near the vehicles, looked their way.

"This should be good right here," Stone said, nodding at the rough-looking men as they passed by.

Renner pulled close to the dark gray, steel, roll-up door of the building next to them and killed the engine. He unlatched his seat and opened his door.

Stone followed suit and stepped out of the passenger side. He moved around the front of the car and across the alley toward the two men. He pointed at Sarah as Renner opened the back door of the squad car.

He reached inside and grabbed her arm.

Sarah stayed put and didn't move, not wanting to budge from her seat.

"Come on. Get out, now." Renner tightened his grip on her bicep. His fingernails bit into her skin. He reached for his collapsible baton.

Sarah scooted across the bench seat and stepped outside of the cruiser.

Renner pulled her away from the car and slammed the door shut. The two men looked her way as Renner escorted her toward them.

Stone shook their hands, looked at Renner, then tilted his head at the entrance of the building. "Let's take her inside, get paid, and get the hell out of here."

One of the guards hung back, staying close to the expensive sedans while the other moved around the trunk toward the entrance.

Renner pulled Sarah to an unknown fate with Stone flanking them. She peered over her shoulder at the portly detective.

Stone diverted his gaze, unwilling to look her in the eye. He put his hand on her back and pushed her along.

Sport-coat pounded his fist against the dull gray door three times, then took a step back.

The door unlocked, then creaked open.

Leatherface emerged from the shadows of the building, then glanced her way. His scarred face contorted in a scowl as he looked her over. "Took you two long enough."

Sarah forced the lump lodged in her throat down. A sickening feeling tormented her gut.

Stone stepped alongside Sarah, then said, "She's a bit slippery, this one. You wanted her undamaged. That took a bit of work."

"So I've noticed. She's killed a number of my men." Leatherface stepped outside, then held the door open. "Take her inside. The boss wants to see her."

I killed his men? What? The statement made little sense to Sarah, seeing as she didn't kill any of them, though, she would've if it meant her living or dying. Spencer dispatched the threats–a detail that Leatherface and his crew had no knowledge of from the sounds of it.

Sport-coat took the lead, followed by Stone. Renner kept a firm hold on Sarah's arm and trailed the men.

Leatherface slammed the door closed behind them, severing the sun from the dark hallway. The men walking before her turned to shadowy figures.

Lights flickered in the distance, then trained toward them. The hollow footfalls echoed in the grim silence. Each step made Sarah's heart pound that much harder.

"Have we not gotten confirmation yet on whether Kinnerk is alive or dead?" The loud, deep voice boomed like thunder down the passageway. "What's taking so damn long? Either he's dead or not. It's not that difficult, Malone."

"Bryce, we're working with our contacts in the police department and men in the area to make this happen. Given the situation with the blackout, and cell service being offline, it has complicated matters a bit," a soft-spoken man replied. "We should know something soon, though."

"I don't give two craps about blackouts or whatever caused this mess. I just want to know if that petty thug is dead or not. We've dismantled a portion of his network already. Cutting the head off the snake is the final blow to making my world better." Bryce's voice grew louder.

The light brightened as numerous lanterns placed around the storage room came into view. Sarah spotted four men standing among the stacks of boxes and steel racks loaded with an array of canned goods and empty pizza boxes.

The chatter among the men ceased as Sport-coat, Stone, and the others came into view.

"Speak of the damn devil and he appears." Bryce threw his large hands in the air. Sweat populated his bullet-shaped head and raced down the sides of his flushed, pudgy cheeks. "Maybe these two will be able to provide some answers instead of giving me excuses."

Stone and Renner stopped with Sarah wedged between them.

Leatherface made a wide arch around the trio. He leaned against the wall in the small open space at the end of the steel rack with his arms folded across his chest.

Stone cleared his throat, then pulled the collar of his button-up shirt away from his neck. "We haven't found anything else out yet, but we're on top of it. As soon as we have something, you'll be the first to know.

"Jesus Christ." Bryce shook his head in disgust. "Guess everyone is failing me. Pathetic."

Stone shifted. "Don't worry, we'll—"

"Don't tell me not to worry." Bryce sounded more like a grizzly bear foaming at the mouth than a man. "Do I need to remind you two of what's at stake if you fail me? With a single order, I could devastate you and your families' worlds. You best remember that."

Neither Renner nor Stone replied.

Sarah quaked in her own skin from the threat, even though it hadn't been directed at her. He spoke as if he could snap his fingers and ruin their lives without much effort.

Bryce looked to Leatherface, then asked, "Is this her? The one Valintino commissioned."

Leatherface chewed on a toothpick and nodded. "Yeah. The mother of the girl Kinnerk's man killed. We weren't able to find her friend at the warehouse either, but we will."

"Make sure of that," Bryce replied. "Have we heard from our inside man, yet? He's late and I'm growing tired of being in this damn sweat box."

"You rang?" a familiar voice sounded from the shadows across the room.

Spencer materialized from the blackness with his white ghost skull mask over his head. He glanced Sarah's way, but acted as though he didn't know her.

Sarah tensed and gulped. Her heart slammed into her throat, and she struggled to catch her breath.

"You're late. And what's up with the mask?" Bryce asked, pointing his thick round finger at him.

"Anonymity," Spencer answered.

"Have you heard anything about Kinnerk? Valintino isn't too thrilled with the sort of heat that's been drummed up because of that hack, and wants us to make sure everything's handled properly from this point on. I'm all too happy to oblige." Bryce spoke with venomous contempt for the rival mobster.

"Nothing yet. Either he's dead and his crew is stalling, or he's alive and ordered them to keep it under wraps. I'm still working it, though." Spencer looked over at Sarah again—a quick glance that no one seemed to catch.

"Work faster. Valintino isn't someone you piss off. His reach is far and so arc his pockets. More than mine. The last thing I need or want is to have his enforcers come after us. They have no problem torturing a man for days. That's one of the main reasons he's one of the big drug lords. We can't muck this up."

Malone looked to Sarah. "So, she's the one who killed our men at the docks and in that alley?"

"Horse shit," Bryce replied, dismissing the question as preposterous. "Look at her. Does she look like she could take out five well-armed men? I think not. I don't care what you say, she had to have help from someone."

"I didn't kill your men," Sarah said, in response to his statement. She looked to Spencer for a second who seemed unafraid by what could come from her mouth.

Renner tugged on her arm, signaling for her to shut her mouth.

"I know you didn't," Bryce replied. "But I imagine you know who did."

Sarah shot Spencer another glance, his name tickling the tip of her tongue. She could oust him right there and be rid of the deviant once and for all, but the irony of her situation left her conflicted.

The one person who tormented her was also the lesser of two evils at the moment.

"I don't. Everything happened so fast that I didn't get a good look at him," Sarah answered.

Bryce ran his large hand over his sweaty face. "We'll see about that. You're not heading off to Valintino just yet. Malone, take her to the other room until we're ready to leave."

Dark Roads

Stone held up his hand, stopping Malone. "With all due respect, I'd like to handle our additional arrangement first before we let her go. We took a risk grabbing her from her home. That is outside the scope we agreed upon."

Malone looked to Bryce, waiting for a response.

"Go ahead and take her. We'll conclude our business with our associates here, so they can get back to protecting these fine streets of Boston."

Stone and Renner moved away from Sarah, allowing Malone to take her.

Spencer kept an eye on her as they walked toward him. "Mind if I tag along? Let them hammer out their business?"

Malone checked with Bryce.

He nodded, then shooed them away.

Spencer waited for them to pass, then walked behind Sarah. They traveled down the narrow hall, lit with lanterns placed against the base of the walls. He leaned in close and whispered into her ear. Sarah shuddered from being so close and feeling his warm breath on her skin. "Wait for my signal, and do as I say if you want to survive this."

CHAPTER TWENTY-FIVE

SARAH

S arah gulped, then swallowed the lump of fear in her throat. Spencer had a plan from the sounds of it, but what could it be?

Kill them and steal her away?

Bargain for her release, or perhaps something else she couldn't think of right then. Either way, he sounded as though he had some sort of idea to get her out.

Malone walked in front of her with Spencer in the back, leading Sarah through the narrow halls and up a flight of stairs.

The discussion between Bryce and the corrupt cops on his payroll faded away, leaving only the sound of their footfalls rapping against each step as they climbed to the second floor.

Two faint reports of gunfire sounded from the way they came.

Dark Roads

Sarah flinched. "What was that?"

"Concluding business, I'd imagine," Malone replied, unshaken by the noise. "Keep moving." He hit the landing of the second floor and skirted past the corner of the wall. The floor creaked under their weight, adding to the eerie ambiance of the building.

A door opened from down the hall. A shadowy figure stepped out into the hallway.

The flickering light illuminated a portion of his stone-cold gaze and his box chin. The grip of a pistol stuck out from the top of his trousers.

Spencer tapped her on the arm, then moved her to the side.

The guard from down the hall reached for his piece, trying to dig it out from his trousers as quick as he could.

Malone stopped and reached inside his sport coat.

A single, muffled report discharged next to her head. Another followed right after.

The guard took two rounds to the chest–center mass. His hold on the weapon fell from his hand and clattered off the floor. He stumbled back into the door jamb, then dropped to the floor.

Malone spun on his heels, and aimed the piece he had clutched tight in his hand.

Spencer shoved Sarah against the wall, clearing her from the line of fire. His gun barked, clipping Malone in his shoulder. The weapon dropped to his side as he groaned in pain.

"What the hell are you doing?" Malone asked, palming the wound on his shoulder. "Bryce is going to have your head for betraying him."

Sarah stayed glued to the wall, shielding her head, and watching the two men battle it out.

"Maybe. Maybe not. Either way, you won't see it," Spencer replied.

Malone lifted his injured arm up, holding the pistol.

Spencer squeezed the trigger, placing a round right between Malone's eyes. His head snapped back and legs buckled, sending him crumbling to the floor.

Sarah removed her arms from around her head, looking at the dead bodies on the floor.

Spencer scanned over the room next to the dead guard, then bent down next to Malone. "You know how to fire one of these, right?"

"Uh, yeah," Sarah replied, a bit shaken.

"Good. You're going to need it." Spencer handed her the piece, then stood up. "Don't shoot me in the back, all right?"

Sarah took the weapon without responding.

Spencer walked past her, then stopped. "Stay close and follow my lead. You see anything move in the shadows, fire until you hear it hit the ground."

Sarah nodded and followed him down the hall toward the staircase. She looked at the back of his masked head, contemplating shooting him now and taking her chances with the men below. Sarah wasn't a cold-blooded killer, though.

Both of her hands clutched the grip of the weapon for dear life as she trailed Spencer down the flight of stairs. Her breathing escalated and her pulse spiked.

A black-clad figure moved in the shadows at the bottom of the staircase. Spencer fired. The shadowy figure fell back into the wall, then down to his back side.

Spencer stepped over the man's lifeless body and turned the corner.

Sarah eyed the man slumped over on his side as she passed by–checking for any sort of movement.

Dark Roads

"So, how exactly do you figure into all of this?" Sarah asked, curious. "I've gathered that you're working both sides, but why?"

"You, Sarah. It's always been about you, but then again, you know how I feel about you," Spencer replied. "But now's not the time. If you want to live, you're just going to have to trust me."

Sarah didn't trust him, but needed him at that moment to escape.

Gunfire rang out from down the corridor. Spencer shielded Sarah with his body, taking a round to the chest. He reeled from the blow, but didn't go down.

Spencer returned fire, popping off multiple shots in quick succession. The gunman from down the hall dropped to his knees, then fell flat on his face.

A hand reached out from behind Sarah, grabbed her shoulder, then spun her around. She squeezed without thought. The bark of the pistol hammered her ears.

"Ah," the man moaned, then shoved her against the wall.

Spencer pulled him off her and placed a round in his temple. The man's body hit the floor with a dull thud. Spencer squeezed the trigger again, but the gun clicked empty. He ejected the spent magazine, retrieved a fresh one from his back pants pocket, and slapped it into the well. He cycled a round, then said, "Come on. We–"

Sarah caught a flash of something moving from the corner of her eye. It hit Spencer in the back and tackled him to the floor.

"I had a feeling it was you," Leatherface said, straddling Spencer's waist. "I told Bryce you couldn't be trusted, but he didn't listen. Guess he will now." Leatherface hammered Spencer's face with his fist, bouncing the back of his skull off of the concrete.

Spencer grabbed his arm and rolled Leatherface to the side. The two men fought on the ground, their bodies tangled as one in the dim light.

Sarah couldn't tell one from the other as the men battled for the upper hand.

Footfalls from down the hallway in the direction they came filled her ears. Panic set in.

Spencer slammed Leatherface's head into the wall, cracking the sheetrock.

The crackle of gunfire boomed in the corridor.

Sarah ducked and returned fire at the two shadowy figures rushing headlong at them.

"Stop firing. You'll hit the woman or me," Leatherface said, through strained breath.

Spencer decked him in the face, loosening Leatherface's hold from around his throat.

Sarah ran, seizing the chance to slip away from both threats. She brought her pistol to bear and swept the hall.

The commotion behind Sarah grew more volcanic–the shouting and slew of threats being tossed about escalated with each passing second.

Sarah craned her neck, looking around the wall for Bryce, his henchmen, or Stone and Renner. Her hand tightened over the grip a hair more as she entered the silent space. She tripped over a body on the floor, and hit the concrete hard.

The pistol popped free of her hand and slid across the ground. Her hand brushed over the floor, searching for the piece.

The light from a lantern tipped over on its side, revealing Stone's bloody face and wide eyes staring at her.

Sarah scooted away from the dead detective on her hands and knees. She ran into a leaning tower of boxes. They tumbled down on top of her. Lost in confusion, and scared out of her mind, Sarah shoved the weighted boxes from her body.

A hand grabbed her arm and jerked her from the floor. Bryce's other right-hand man who had stood next to Malone held onto her tight.

Sarah jammed the heel of her palm into his nose, then kicked him in the groin. She grabbed what hair she could find on his head and rammed her knee into his face.

His arms went wide as he fell back onto Stone.

Her foot moved and hit something solid.

Sarah dipped her chin and searched the floor. Her piece sat just to the right of her.

Bryce's man reached inside his coat, retrieving his sidearm from the shoulder holster. He pulled it out just as Sarah got her hands on the grip of hers.

She turned and fired, squeezing the trigger twice without thought.

Two rounds hammered his chest. His arm went limp, dropping the gun to the floor.

Sarah skirted past the round table Bryce and his men stood around, heading for the hallway that led out to the alley. Bryce had vanished, gone from the building as far as she could tell.

Another dead body laid face first on the concrete near the entrance to the dark hallway. The scant bit of light that reached the body revealed the officer's uniform. Renner.

The hammering of footsteps charged from the other hall. Sarah turned on her heels and looked, but couldn't see around the blind corner. She stooped down and riffled through Renner's pockets, frantic to find the keys to his squad car.

Come on. Come on.

The jagged edge caught the tips of her fingers. She pulled them out. The footfalls drew closer.

Sarah turned and fired down the hall, running on pure instinct and a will to survive. She stood and ran the length of the hall in a flash, focusing on the door.

The footfalls chased Sarah down like a predator after its prey. She plowed through the door without breaking her stride and swept the alley.

One of the luxury sedans had left, leaving the other behind.

Sarah sprinted around the rear of the BMW and charged the cruiser. The keys fumbled in her hands as she neared the driver's side. She threw open the door and dropped down into the seat. Her mind worked a mile a minute while her hands sifted through the keys.

There.

A flash of movement caught the corner of her eye. She slipped the key into the ignition. The engine came to life. Spencer rushed the squad car with his mask clutched in his hand. His mouth moved, but she couldn't make out what he screamed at her.

Sarah shifted into drive, then punched the gas as he neared the door.

His hand hammered the window–eyes focused on her as he ran alongside the car. "Sarah. Stop and open the–"

The cruiser pulled away and took off down the alley. She glanced in the rear-view mirror, took a deep breath, and watched Spencer chase after her full tilt.

The squad car pulled away, leaving her stalker behind and Sarah thankful to be alive.

Dark Roads

CHAPTER TWENTY-SIX

RUSSELL

The two-lane road snaked through blind corners and sharp turns, testing Clyde's attention span and ability to navigate the winding road.

"Where's this place at?" Clyde asked, pushing his Chevy truck hard through each turn. He worked the brake and gas in tandem, drifting around each bend at harrowing speeds. The tires hugged the road, fighting to stay out of the ditch.

Russell struggled to think straight as he worried about what might be happening to Cathy. If anything more happened to her, he wouldn't be able to forgive himself. "Um, it's some old creepy house down a gravel road. We cut through a field to get into town because of those whack jobs, so nothing looks familiar."

"I'm going to need a bit more than that, friend, or we're just spinning our wheels and wasting time," Clyde replied.

Dark Roads

Max laid on the back seat with his head draped over his front paws, staring at both men.

Russell peered through the windshield, spotting the rolling hills in the far distance. The dense woods next to the road passed by the pickup, jogging his memory. "Yeah, this is the right way, I think. We cut through those woods there that dumped us out into an open field. There should be a gravel road up ahead as long as we haven't passed it already."

"I haven't seen any gravel road yet, so I think we're good." Clyde kept his rifle in the floorboard between his leg and the center console. It slid toward Russell. Clyde removed his hand from the steering wheel and grabbed the long barrel to keep it steady. "Don't worry. We'll make it there in time."

The Chevy crested the hill of the road, then rolled down the other side.

"Hold on. I think I see the gravel road ahead of us." Russell pointed to the weeds and other verdure that lined the east side of the road.

Clyde nodded. "I see it. Hold on."

He punched the brake, then spun the steering wheel counterclockwise. The back end of the truck swung wide. A loud rattling noise of the items stowed in the back banged off the walls of the bed and filled the cab.

"This is it. The house should be up on our right. Not sure how far it is, though," Russell said.

A large cloud of dust lifted into the air from the pickup barreling over the gravel road. Rocks caught within the tread of the tires pelted the undercarriage.

"How many men are you expecting to be there besides the ones that left in that SUV?" Clyde asked.

"Not sure. Counting the two men we encountered out on the road, plus the SUV, I'd say four or so. Maybe more. I don't know," Russell answered. "I plan for the worst and hope for the best, though."

"You got a gun?" Clyde asked.

Russell shook his head. "Nope. Had a six shooter that I took off one of Ty's men, but it's bone dry and back in town."

Clyde pointed at the glove compartment. "Pop that open. I've got a .38 Special in there you can use. It's got five rounds loaded. I hope that'll be enough."

Max groaned, then leaned over the center console between the two men. He looked out of the windshield, panting with his tongue hanging out. He licked at Russell's face, catching the side of his cheek.

"You doing all right, bud?" Russell rubbed his head, then popped open the glove compartment.

The snub nose revolver rattled about in the oversized bin.

"Don't let the size fool you. That bad boy will pack a punch. Plus, it's super easy to conceal," Clyde said, as if to sell the gun's capabilities.

Russell grabbed the weapon and closed the open lid. He looked over the modest revolver, then popped out the cylinder, finding it fully stocked and ready to go. "To be honest, I'd be happy with just about anything."

The house came into view between the trees that lined the rocky road. The black SUV and Corona's truck sat in the driveway next to the large, old home.

Clyde spotted it as well, then pointed through the windshield. "Is that it?"

"Yeah. You might want to slow some and park on the side of the road here," Russell replied. "I'd rather them think they aren't going to have any company than for them to be ready for us."

"Agreed." Clyde parked half of the truck in the ditch and behind a wall of thick bushes and trees. He killed the engine and removed the keys from the ignition. "What's our game plan?"

Russell rubbed his stubbled chin, trying to formulate a plan of attack. Not knowing where the men were or their actual strength made it difficult to say. Plus, he just wanted to go full bore, and get to Cathy as fast as possible. "We can take the back of the house if you want to take the front, or we can all just stick together and hit the back."

Clyde opened his door. "We'll figure it out. Come on."

Russell pushed open the passenger side door.

Max hopped over the center console and followed him out to the weeds. The German shepherd moved a bit sluggishly, but looked ready enough to handle business.

Clyde held his rifle tight as they stalked through the weeds and along the line of rich verdure that lined the road. He paused, shouldered the rifle, then peered through the scope mounted on the top.

"See any movement outside?" Russell asked, standing at his two o'clock.

"I've got eyes on two men heading back into the house," Clyde answered. "Other than that, I don't see any other movement, but they could be around the back side of the home as well." Clyde lowered the rifle.

Russell studied the house for a moment longer. "Let's go. I need to get inside of there."

They double timed it down the road, keeping out of sight of the home as much as possible.

Max galloped with a limp, but charged full steam ahead.

They paused at the entrance of the driveway, skimmed over the windows and area around the house, then worked their way up toward the home.

Russell grabbed the small handle of the .38 Special with both hands, ready to save his friend's life by any means necessary.

"I'll go ahead and take the front if you want to take the back of the house," Clyde said, nodding at the derelict porch that wrapped around the front.

"That'll work."

Clyde broke away, keeping low, and raced toward the edge of the porch.

Russell and Max moved along the side of the SUV, then down the truck. He grabbed Max by the collar, then peered over the hood toward the enclosed porch.

John Deere stood on the walkway near the steps, puffing on a cigarette. Smoke escaped from his mouth as he stared off into the field past the ramshackle garage.

Russell didn't spot a weapon, but that didn't mean he didn't have one on him.

Max inched forward, but Russell grabbed him by the collar.

"Hold on. I've got an idea." Russell whistled just loud enough so that John Deere would hear it.

John Deere looked their way, then craned his neck, searching for the noise. He took one last deep drag, then discarded the cigarette on the grass. He walked toward the truck, pulling the pistol tucked in his waistband.

Russell waited to make his move, allowing him to get within range. He dropped to the ground and hid behind the oversized tire of the truck. He peered under the pickup, watching John Deere come closer.

Dark Roads

Max growled and inched forward. Each crunch of the rocks under his boots sent him further on edge. A subtle growl loomed from his throat and chest.

John Deere stopped shy of the front end. He stood there for a moment, then turned around, but didn't move.

Russell looked around the bumper as John Deere lit another cigarette. Thin trails of smoke trailed above his head.

John Deere pocketed his lighter and tilted his head back, savoring the scent of the rich tobacco stick.

Russell moved around the pickup, stalking the vile man. He kept low and closed in fast. He wrapped his arms around the man's neck and covered his mouth with his hand, knocking the cigarette from his lips.

"Remember me, asshole?" Russell asked, whispering in his ear. He dragged him back to the far side of the truck.

John Deere flung his arms out, screaming for help.

Russell flexed his arm under the man's chin and kept the palm of his hand pressed to his mouth. He squeezed tight. John Deere gasped for air and clawed at his forearm. His body went limp after a few moments of thrashing about.

Russell sat him on the ground.

Max sniffed the body and growled, baring his fangs at the unconscious man.

Russell grabbed his piece from the ground and stuffed it into his waistband. They made for the back porch in a flash. The bronco tilted to the side. Russell didn't recall the tires be lowing on air and figured Ty and his men must've slashed the tires. Great. He swept the area, climbed the concrete steps, then opened the screen door.

Max pushed past him, sniffing the floor.

Russell eyed the closed door leading into the kitchen. The dull lighting and the layer of grime on the window made it hard to see any movement in the kitchen.

Max paused, trained his attention at the door, then growled.

Russell closed the door and hurried across the porch to the wall on the side of the door. He caught a flash of movement through the window. The rotted planks of wood creaked under his bulk, making him cringe.

The doorknob jiggled. The door opened.

"Ned, is that you?" Corona asked from inside the kitchen.

A crackle of gunfire echoed from the front of the house, followed by screams of panic.

Corona turned with his back to the porch. "What the–"

Max attacked. He latched onto Corona's wrist and dragged him out onto the porch.

"Jesus Christ." Corona dropped the pistol in his hand, then punched Max in the face. Panted breaths fled his mouth.

Each blow only enraged the German shepherd more. He thrashed his head, ripping and tearing through the hairy flesh of Corona's forearm.

Russell clipped Corona on the jaw with his fist–knocking him hard to the floor.

Corona hit with a dense thump.

Max ravaged his mangled limb, biting and clawing at his arm.

He left the canine to deal with Corona, then charged inside the home with the revolver up and at the ready. Shouting loomed from the living room where he'd left Cathy. Bright flashes of muzzle fire signaled the positions of the men.

Russell swept the kitchen and charged down the hallway. Bright light shone from the room across from the living room, illuminating the foyer.

Dark Roads

Black Mustache skirted the banister of the staircase in a panic, his hand palming his arm. His piece hung at his side, finger over the trigger. He spotted Russell, then tried to lift his injured arm.

Russell pulled the trigger of the snub-nosed revolver. It barked. Fire spat from the shortened barrel. A single round punched through Black Mustache's stomach.

Max tore past Russell and lunged at the wounded man, taking him down by his hand.

Three down, Russell thought, hoping to only have two more to contend with.

Clyde appeared from the room to his left with his rifle shouldered.

Russell moved his gun, but held fire.

"I got one in there." Clyde glanced down at Max who worked on Black Mustache. "I shot him in the arm."

"We took out two more out back. That should hopefully leave–"

A dense thud sounded from the living room, followed by a crashing noise. Russell charged ahead, past the staircase with Clyde at his side. Max trailed the two men as they entered the living room with weapons hot.

Cathy had Ty pinned to the floor, straddling his waist near the fireplace. He rolled his hips and pushed at her shoulders, trying to get her off of him.

Russell sprinted across the living room with Max in tow.

Ty knocked Cathy to the floor, then scrambled to his feet. He struggled to keep his balance and leaned at the fireplace.

Cathy rolled to her back, then took aim with the 9mm clutched in her hands. She squeezed the trigger, firing off three rounds in quick succession, hitting Ty center mass.

Max rushed to her side, growling and baring his fangs at the last remaining threat.

Ty's legs gave as he dropped to the floor. He gurgled on his own blood as Russell closed in. Blood seeped from the wounds to the dusty wooden planks. Ty looked up at Russell, each breath shallower than the last as he faded away.

Cathy groaned as Max attacked her face with his tongue. "There's my boy." She hugged around his neck, then kissed the side of his head.

"Are you all right?" Russell asked, looking her over for any signs of trauma.

"Yeah. Minus a busted lip, sore ribs, and my throbbing leg, I'm peachy." Cathy noticed Clyde, then asked, "Who is he?"

Clyde lowered the rifle. "Clyde McNab."

"He helped us out and got us back here after we ran into these guys in town." Russell pulled the rucksack from his shoulders and unzipped the top. "There aren't any more of the them inside, are there?"

Cathy laid there, then said, "Not that I'm aware of. Our two friends from the highway went outside."

"Yeah. We took care of them." Russell pulled out the medical supplies and pain meds. "Here. I got some pills that should help with the pain."

"Thanks." Cathy popped the top and downed two of the pills.

Russell tended to her gunshot wound, cleaning and wrapping it with gauze. "All right. You should be good to go, now."

Max sat on his haunches next to her, watching Russell tend to her wound.

"Can we get out of here now and back on the road," she asked. "I've had my fill of dirty, disgusting rednecks."

Dark Roads

"We're not leaving in the Bronco. They slashed the tires and that radiator is still screwed," Russell said. "We could take one of their rides. Preferably the SUV since it looks newer and will probably be more comfortable."

"Where are you heading?" Clyde asked, securing the rifle over his shoulder.

"Philly to get her daughter," Russell answered. "Then, on to Boston so I can get back to my wife."

"Why don't the three of you ride with me, and I'll take you?" Clyde said, looking at Russell, then down at Cathy. "I don't have anything else waiting for me at home, and you need the help."

"Are you sure? You've already done a lot for us, and you don't really even know us," Russell said.

Clyde nodded. "Yeah. I'm sure. You helped me stop the people I'd been hunting and got some justice for my wife. Maybe I can be of some help along the way. Besides, with the way things are right now, and your friend hurt, might not be a bad idea to have some back up in case the shit hits the fan again."

Cathy pushed Max away, then wiggled her hands at the two men towering over her. They each took a hand, pulling her from the floor. She favored her wounded leg, then leaned back against the brick surface of the fireplace. "I don't care what vehicle we take or who comes with us. I just want to get out of here, make it to my daughter, and find your wife."

Russell couldn't agree more. He needed to get back on the road and home to his wife. To his love.

255

Derek Shupert

ABOUT THE AUTHOR

Derek Shupert is an emerging Science Fiction Author known for his captivating dystopian storylines and post-apocalyptic-laden plots. With various books and anthologies underway, he is also the author of the Afflicted series and Sentry Squad.

Outside of the fantastical world of sci-fi, Derek serves as the Vice President at Woodforest National Bank. During his free time, he enjoys reading, exercising, and watching apocalyptic movies and TV shows like Mad Max and The Walking Dead. Above all, he is a family man who cherishes nothing more than quality time spent with his loved ones.

To find out more about Derek Shupert and his forthcoming publications, visit his official website at **www.derekshupert.com.**

Printed in Great Britain
by Amazon

33594836R00152